READING, 'RITING, AND RUTHLESSNESS

READING, 'RITING, AND RUTHLESSNESS

CYNTHIA MURRAY

ISBN-13: 978-1500435684
ISBN-10: 1500435686

Cover Photo by Getty Images
Cover Design by Angie_ProCovers

For my sons, H. J. and G. Murray Boykin,
with love and gratitude

In the first place, God made idiots. That was for practice. Then he made school boards.

—Mark Twain

Never doubt that a small group of thoughtful and committed citizens can change the world….

—Margaret Mead

CHAPTER 1

"No! You can't be serious!"

I shouted in response to my colleague, Louise Ryan.

What she had just told me was unbelievable. She apparently had only just learned from one of her contacts that we, the psychologists for the school district, were going to be evicted from our offices with little or no warning. Now Louise was in the process of sharing that horrible forecast with me. My reaction was one of total disbelief.

"On the sidewalk! Our offices … on the sidewalk? What! You have got to be kidding!"

I was experiencing complete shock and anxious uncertainty.

Louise was my friend and fellow psychologist. She had stumbled upon this critical information in talking with one of her distant relatives, who was a school district maintenance worker, and knew at once that she had to tell me what was being planned.

Bottom line: The incoming superintendent, Dr. Jane Smith, was clearing the three psychologists – Louise, Ashley Howe, and me, Claire Franklin – out of the school district administration building.

We had no place to go.

We couldn't go to one of the elementary or secondary schools. They didn't have room for us. Besides, we were district level professionals, not building level. And anyway, that would be too humiliating, too embarrassing.

We understood only too well that the administration building for a public school district represents the hub of power and influence in the educational community. In some places it is referred to as the Board of Education.

This essential center of operations and power is also called the district office – the D.O. That term, though, is somewhat misleading because it serves not as one office, but as the home base for a complex of different offices and departments including the superintendent, assistant superintendents, the various department directors, and instructional coordinators for the school district.

The fact that our offices were in the administration building meant that the psychologists were a part of the district level sphere of influence as opposed to being 'building level' or a part of an individual school. We were each assigned to provide services to four or five schools out in the school district, but our offices were at the district office. This arrangement allowed us to provide centralized quality psychological services in spite of the fact that we were woefully understaffed.

It was important for the psychologists to be based at the D.O. Having offices in the administration building symbolized the status that we were afforded by the entire school community by virtue of being housed with the district's powerful educational elite.

The three of us – Louise, Ashley and I – had been psychologists for Dane County School District at the beginning of the 1990-91 school year. We were all doctoral level. I was, and continue to be, the only African-American psychologist in the district.

Ashley and I were close in age, in our mid-forties, but she was married and I was a divorced mother of two sons. The third psychologist, Louise, was older, in her fifties, and presented herself in such a manner that she came across as a mature, experienced professional, due in part to the fact that her stylish, close-cut hair remained a natural shade of gray.

One of Louise's strengths was her practical nature. She tried not to leave anything to chance if she could help it. Not surprisingly, in this situation, she had already spoken about our plight with a long-time family friend who was also a district administrator. Out of this conversation came a potential site for the psychologists to use as a new home. We would be going from upper echelon at the district office to the vocational center.

And we thought Dr. Smith had done the worst thing to us that she could when she moved our offices from the second floor to the basement of the D.O. Wrong! Now we were being tossed on the street and the only place that had room for us was the vocational center. Who would believe such a thing?

I remember several years earlier when news of the forced move of the psychologists to the basement spread over the school district, there were a lot of jokes and not-so-nice comments. One assistant principal told me that word in the schools was that the only reason we were in the basement was because there wasn't a lower level. Well now Jane Smith had found it.

Forget the basement.

Forget the schools.

Our only option was the district's vocational center. No question of tier now. We had been banished to the district's Vocational-Technical Center, commonly referred to as Vo-Teck.

❖

Just last week before the school board meeting to name Dr. Jane Smith as the new superintendent, Louise and I had gone early so that we could sit in our offices in the basement to discuss the recent events. I recall that I remained downstairs on the phone with one of our contacts after Louise went up to find seats.

Later, as I started upstairs, I ran into John Dye, the head of Food Services and Maintenance for the district. His office was directly across the hall from ours and we both ended up heading to the board meeting at the same time. After we said hello, he became uncharacteristically talkative with me, which was the exact opposite of the normally taciturn person that I had grown to know over several years. He dropped his eyes and commented that he would be glad when the next day was finally over.

"Why?" I questioned immediately.

John's reply wasn't anything like what I expected. I thought that he was going to say that he would be glad because it would mean that the first day for the school district with Dr. Smith at the helm would be over. Instead, I found his response to be even more perplexing. What he said was that he didn't want to have to deal with all the "bitching". I was already surprised that he was engaging in any type of conversation with me, but his use of the b-word was so unexpected that I forgot to ask who or what he was referring to with his comments.

The statements that John made, as he continued to talk, answered my unspoken questions. He shared information which turned out later to be quite meaningful in terms of what eventually happened to the psychologists. He said that all of the women were going to start bitching about the changes that Dr. Smith was going to make.

I felt strangely uneasy as he told me that. "Women? What women are you talking about?" I stopped and looked at him.

"The secretaries."

John kept walking briskly and I had to almost run to catch up with him again. "Oh ... but you mentioned changes. What kind of changes?"

Then he really added to the puzzle because he shook his head with a frown on his face and said, "Uh-uh. That's not anything that I can tell you."

"Why not?" I didn't think he was being fair at this point to suddenly withhold information.

"I probably should not have said anything at all. But I definitely can't tell you what's going to happen." He didn't say another word.

By this time we were already upstairs on the first floor and had walked down the long hall to the boardroom on the other end.

As John and I entered the boardroom, we split up. He went in one direction and I went in another after stopping briefly near the door and scanning the room to look for Louise. The boardroom was crowded. It seemed that everyone in Dane County and half of South Carolina had turned out for the coronation.

When I located Louise, I went over and automatically sat in the vacant chair beside her. I couldn't wait to quickly repeat what John had said.

Almost before she could say anything about my conversation with John, I rapidly fired off some questions:

"Do you think we'll have to move?"

"Do you think that's what he's talking about?"

Then I began to answer my own questions. "Probably not, because he gave me the impression he was only talking about the secretaries. I'll bet that's it … it's just the secretaries."

Louise opined that since we were professionals, surely we would have heard something more than the rumors floating around among the maintenance workers.

For some reason we overlooked the obvious; John was the district's maintenance director. The rumors were coming from maintenance workers. In retrospect, we probably should have realized the connection that night. We didn't.

But then, we had to stop speculating. The board meeting was being called to order.

Dr. Jane Smith was sitting at the head of the large conference table, near the far end of the room, waiting to assume her duties formally as leader of the school district. To her right was seated the school board chairman, her longtime friend, Celeste Washington, an attractive, distinguished looking, almost regal, woman whose youthful appearance belied her age. Celeste had weathered many storms since becoming the first African-American to chair the trustee board. She was a strong advocate for children and schools and was known for her desire to treat everyone fairly, regardless of color or socio-economic status. She conducted herself in such a professional, yet compassionate manner that she easily earned the respect of not only her constituents in the black community, but other county residents as well. She was able to instill the element of trust in most people who met her.

Celeste loved the power of being at the head of the county school board. She definitely enjoyed wielding the gavel. The recognition and prestige were great perks. And now tonight, after over a decade of service, she was going to formally help her friend, Dr. Jane Smith, assume her new position. She was actually going to swear Jane in as superintendent – the first female superintendent for the school district.

Ah, things appeared to be going so well. It was less than a year ago that the board was having contentious meetings with citizens up in arms protesting the prospect of Jane becoming district superintendent. Who would have thought that the controversies surrounding Jane Smith would die out and the community would stop fighting so hard to keep her from the school district's top leadership position.

❖

As my thoughts flitted about that night in the school board meeting on all that had transpired in the past, they naturally landed on Ashley Howe, the other psychologist who occupied the third office on the end in our suite.

Ashley and I were hired by the school district the same year. Since I had been with the district a few weeks before she interviewed, I managed to be a part of the informal committee which recommended her to the director of Special Services. She was one of two graduate students who applied for the position opening, but the secretary and I preferred her to the other psychologist. We thought she was much more personable and had a great smile. After being hired as a psychologist for the school district, she moved to Dane County with her husband and son, a preschooler.

For ten years, Ashley and I worked together exceptionally well in Dane County School District. We were similar philosophically in our goal of providing a full array of services to students, teachers, administrators, and parents. We viewed our jobs as more than testing. Neither one of us saw anything wrong with wearing as many hats as necessary to be certain that students' needs were being met. We had been a great team on many projects and issues during those years.

Ashley and I had often jogged or walked together at one of the county exercise trails. Although it was never planned, we occasionally ran into each other and would end up exercising at the same time. We jokingly acknowledged that the physical activity helped us deal with job stress related to Jane Smith.

In the year and a half before Ashley left, we both had managed to get the inevitable battle scars from our individual encounters with our supervisor, Jane Smith. The main thing that Jane took issue with, involving me, was how much time she claimed I spent doing someone else's job. She did not want me to facilitate, or assist with, what she considered to be activities that should be in the province of a social worker. Her attitude was that I was a hopeless do-gooder forever trying to 'be all things for all children'.

Once Jane Smith became our supervisor, she made procedural changes to curtail specific duties that she decided should be handled by other district personnel. Her approach to supervising the psychologists was to micromanage certain aspects of our jobs and to ignore others. She would only keep up with evaluations in schools where the administrator was a friend or political ally. I remember at one point I went by her office to discuss the testing caseload. Jane took a sheet of paper from her desk and read the names of students that I had tested at Riverplains Elementary, where she had formerly been principal. I was stunned. The assistant principal was her protégée and was apparently reporting my activities in the school to her on a regular basis, which was highly unusual.

❖

How Jane even came to supervise the psychologists is a long story, but the short version is that as the Assistant Superintendent of Instructional Services, she managed to convince the superintendent that the three psychologists would be more productive if they were placed under her supervision. For reasons never fully explained to us, the decision was then made to change the psychologists from Special Services to Instructional Services. The department change occurred on the same morning that we were forced to move from the second floor to the basement without any prior warning. All of this was two years before Jane became superintendent.

On the morning of the move I was awakened at home by a phone call from Celeste Washington notifying me of the proposed change only hours before it took place.

"I thought you knew that we were planning to put you under Jane," Celeste said.

I was still sleepy and trying to process the information. It felt as though the world had shifted as I slept and now that I was awake, I was trying to get my bearings and make sense of it all.

"How would I know something like that?" I asked.

Celeste replied, "It was being talked about in the district."

"You mean our director of Special Services knew about it?"

"Of course, she knew. We thought she would talk it over with the psychologists. She never said anything to you?"

"Not a word. She never told me anything. She may have said something to Ashley Howe, but I had no idea something like this was going to happen."

"I know that it was discussed in the Cedar Hills area."

"Cedar Hills? Celeste, that's way on the other end of the county. How would I know what was being said in Cedar Hills? I don't have any schools out there. I never get out there. No one told me anything."

"I'm sorry, but I couldn't say anything until after the board approved the change. We did that in our meeting last night."

"Well thank you for letting me know. I guess they'll give us the details when I get to work this morning."

Awake or not, it wasn't until I actually got to work that the impact and ramifications of the move hit me. Special Services was in mourning. I sensed the feeling of grief, of loss, as I walked into the department. It was a very emotionally draining experience for us all. The only thing that the director would tell us was that the move had to be made that morning and she was not permitted to elaborate or discuss it with us. She gave us the impression that the only way that she could hold on to her was job was to let us go. She chose not to fight Jane Smith.

The official rationale from the administration for relocating us to the basement was that the psychologists couldn't stay on the second floor with Special Services if they were going to now be under Instructional Services.

The change was nothing short of drastic.

Psychologists in the school district provide a variety of functions that range from consultations and interventions in the classroom to chairing meetings and developing instructional programs for special education students. Nevertheless, our primary role in the school district continued to be conducting psychoeducational evaluations of students for possible special education services. In so doing, we served as gatekeepers for special education. Clearly it was a perversion of the way we provided services to take us from special education when we were so closely aligned.

However, the move was slightly more palatable when we put a positive spin on it. That way we could emphasize that we went from answering to a department director to being supervised by an assistant superintendent. From that perspective, it was actually a promotion of sorts.

CHAPTER 2

When the word got out that Jane Smith was in line for the superintendency, Ashley and I spent considerable time exchanging and sharing information from the schools. We often watched the key players in the saga coming and going from our vantage point in the basement.

In spite of the fact that I had just relocated back to South Carolina and Dane County the first year we worked together, I was originally from the area and saw myself as being more involved in the community over time than Ashley. For example, I served on a county board for the disabled and was appointed to a state level board for children in foster care. As far as the school district was concerned, I attended school board meetings regularly and thought that I knew far more about the mood in the district than she did. Ashley didn't go to board meetings and didn't have contact with board members or local politicians the way I did. I remember saying to her one day, "There is no way the parents and voters of Lucien Heights, or Dane

County for that matter, are going to allow Jane become superintendent."

"I know you keep up with the political buzz, Claire, but you've missed it this time. My gut feeling is that she will become superintendent."

I couldn't believe she said that. It sounded to me like something she heard from a principal or a person in the schools who supported Jane. "Is that your gut feeling or did someone close to the administration tell you that?"

Ashley snapped back, "It doesn't matter, the board is going to name her superintendent."

She didn't seem to understand. "Ashley you haven't been to any of the board meetings when the parents are expressing their opposition. Feelings run high in those meetings."

"But those people don't have any power and the average person doesn't care what happens with the school district," she asserted.

"I don't believe that. I think that the people of this county will march with protest signs out in front of this building before they will allow her to become superintendent."

"No I think you're wrong this time. You'll see. Jane is going to be the next superintendent."

"No way."

Although I was convinced there existed a solid base of opposition from throughout the county, Ashley had me concerned enough that I decided to take a chance and approach Louise to get her opinion about Jane's chances.

When Louise first came back to the district, it was about two years before Dr. Smith became superintendent and one year after our department, Psychological Services, had been moved to the basement. It was rumored that Jane had been responsible for Louise coming back. I heard at the time that they had been close friends politically and socially for many years. Coincidentally, Louise had left the district to go to graduate school just as I had relocated to Dane County from another part of the state. So we had not worked together before and she missed out on that first major move of the psychologists.

I tried to be tactful when I approached Louise with the question, "Louise, I know that you and Jane are close, so I was wondering what you think about all of the controversy surrounding her attempt to become superintendent."

Unbeknownst to me, things had changed and Louise did not mince words in letting me know, speaking in her customary slow, deliberate manner.

"Claire, I can see I need to bring you up to date. Jane and I are not close anymore. We haven't been for some time. She is moving up these days and is clearly determined to leave some of us behind. And to answer your question … no, quite frankly I don't think Jane will become superintendent. She spends most of her time now trying to cater to that downtown crowd. I guess she thinks that will help her achieve her goal."

"But, those are the very people who don't want her to become superintendent. They're her strongest opposition."

"I know, but she thinks she can get them on her side."

"What do you think?"

Louise squinted and gave me hard look before answering. "I don't think she can. I think she's fighting a losing battle. Years ago it was her husband, Junior, who wanted to be superintendent and now it's Jane. They're just keeping it in the family."

"I told Ashley that I can see the voters marching in front of the D.O. and carrying protest signs before they'll let it happen."

"Naaw, they won't march in Dane County. There's not enough concern. Those of us who are talking about it care what happens with the school district because we're in it everyday – we work for the district and we're caught up in it, but most people don't give a rip about the school district."

"Ashley said the same thing."

"She's right."

❖

Ashley seemed convinced that Jane would become superintendent, but I still thought she was mistaken. She had not attended any of the raucous, acrimonious board meetings of late. I had. For that reason alone, I felt confident that she did not understand Dane County politics, especially school district politics.

The meetings had started changing from being rather mundane and fairly boring affairs near the time word got out that Dr. Jane Smith had the superintendency in hand. The majority of people in the county may not have paid that much attention, but there was a group of parents who took notice. These parents were from an upscale section of downtown Lucien Heights and were well educated and active in school district affairs. As soon as that group heard Jane was planning to automatically replace the outgoing superintendent, they became even more active and vocal.

Some of the people in the county referred to the downtown parents as the 'downtown clique'. The clique began putting the talents and resources they had available to use in fighting Jane Smith through the proper channels. They talked to their board members, attended board meetings, and scheduled appointments to see the outgoing superintendent in conference. When it appeared that they were not making as much progress as they hoped, they turned it up a notch. The clique was well aware that the board listened to the public in meetings, if for no other reason than the local paper, the *Lucien Heights Herald,* might carry a story and each board member wanted to go on record as coming across in a favorable manner.

Once the clique demonstrated more interest in board activities by faithfully attending the sessions, the school board meetings changed noticeably. There was more focus and organization. The agenda was suddenly meaningful. It became more than just a way to look conscientious and keep up appearances for about two hours. There were indications that the board members were reviewing their board packets before meetings. They were no longer simply sitting and sifting through the packet after the meeting started to try to look interested or keep from falling asleep. They gave the appearance of truly understanding that there was a purpose for the board packets and that they had a responsibility to at least become familiar with the information contained within those packets prior to the meetings.

The members of the clique rotated board meetings. That is, there were rarely all members of the group attending a particular meeting at the same time. It was well thought out and clearly well planned.

I attended board meetings during that time to stay current with board activities and also to help add diversity to the meetings. Celeste and I were usually the only African-Americans at the meetings, but she was on the board. That meant that I was typically the only person of color sitting among the members of the clique.

When the opposition began to heat up concerning Jane becoming superintendent, my mother, Mildred Christianson, who was a retired teacher, suggested that I follow her good friend, Celeste, home after the meetings to make sure that she got in safely. Celeste thought that it was a good idea and told me that she appreciated it.

By attending the school board meetings in the period before Jane became superintendent, I got to know many of the downtown clique members. The level of education in the clique as a whole surpassed that of the board, collectively. A number of the clique members had post graduate degrees and one stay-at-home mom had her law degree. The lawyer mom, Mootsie Daniels, provided valuable assistance in questions of school law and state law. There were times when the clique needed advice in one or both areas and Mootsie readily did the research and then gave the group a legal opinion. I remember that after one of the meetings she spoke to all of us – I was associating with them – about our chances of a recall election since the board was turning a deaf ear on the group. It was from the lawyer mom, Mootsie, that we learned that South Carolina law did not have any provision for recalling elected officials. They could be impeached, under certain conditions, but they could not be recalled.

The message for us was that we were stuck with the members who were on the school board at that time until later when they were up for reelection. The board seats were staggered which meant that we could elect or defeat only 50% of the board members every two years. We had just reelected four of the board members and wouldn't have another chance for at least two more years. By that time,

Jane would have been superintendent for two years. That was not anything anyone in the clique wanted to have to live with if it could be avoided.

❖

With so many people opposed to Jane Smith showing up at each board meeting and speaking out against her as superintendent, the board decided to hold a public forum to give everyone a chance to voice his or her opinion about Jane becoming the next superintendent and to presumably put the matter to rest. The forum was scheduled, as it turned out, on the coldest day of the year. It was held at the Vo-Teck auditorium at 7:00 a.m. on a Saturday morning.

People could not believe that the board would stoop so low as to schedule a public forum for 7:00 in the morning. Their strategy was so transparent. The board thought that people would not come out at that time in the morning just to oppose Jane. They were wrong. I was even willing to forego sleeping in that Saturday morning so that I could be at Vo-Teck and witness the event.

People came in droves.

The Vo-Teck auditorium has the largest seating capacity of any of the school venues in the district. Yet that Saturday morning there was not enough room. There were wall-to-wall people of all ages from tiny babies in parents' arms to the elderly who were assisted by family members. There were approximately 30 to 35 African-Americans in attendance giving the meeting good representation from the black community. I sat in the back of the auditorium, which was elevated, primarily in order to have a good vantage point to witness the proceedings. The moderator for the forum came from out of town and was a consultant from the state school board association. The board members sat on the stage and never had to do anything other than try to stay awake and pay attention. The moderator was completely in charge of the forum.

People were allowed to speak without having to sign in or to take a number. They simply had to raise their hands. The loosely structured format worked well for the public that morning. There was a willingness on the part of the assemblage to give everyone a chance to voice his or her opinion. One of Junior Smith's staff from his elementary school, a secretary, was sitting on the upper level on the other side of the auditorium across from my area. Although both Junior and Jane were present, the secretary apparently had been directed to take names and keep notes on everything that was said.

My estimate was that approximately 80 to 90 percent of the people at the forum were opposed to Jane Smith. The speakers generally felt that Jane was not qualified or at the very least was not the best-qualified person for the job.

The first speaker was a young woman who stated, "I am a parent of three school age children. I have known Jane Smith almost all of my life. She was controversial when she was principal at Riverplains Elementary and I think that she will bring that kind of notoriety to the whole district if she is named superintendent." The woman was probably referring to the public perception that Jane had undermined her predecessor and forced the poor man to retire so that she could become principal at Riverplains Elementary School.

An elderly man accompanied his wife to the microphone evidently to support her when she spoke. "This is no offense against Dr. Smith, but I think we need someone with better qualifications."

The man's contribution was much more detailed than his wife's. "I think that the board should conduct a nation-wide search for the new superintendent. The district would be better off with someone who can come in with new ideas in education and running schools."

A businessman from the downtown clique asserted, "If Jane Smith becomes superintendent, it will be a slap in the face of every citizen of Dane County. Dr. Smith will continue the 'good old boy' politics and she'll use her position to further her own personal interests and not work for the good of the school district."

Still another downtown clique member had different concerns. "The children of Dane County deserve someone with expertise in educational administration and with some prior experience as a superintendent. Dr. Smith will have to be given on the job training. The children deserve better."

A man who identified himself as from the Riverplains area was worried about PR for Dane County. "The county needs someone who can represent them as a top notch educator at the state and regional level. Can Dr. Smith do that?"

Many people suggested looking outside Dane County as typified by these comments. "I want the school board to know that this district needs to look outside of Dane County and find someone with a proven track record in administration and impeccable credentials. We don't need to settle for less."

A good old boy type stated what he thought was obvious. "I believe, 'If it ain't broke, don't fix it'. There's nothing wrong with our current superintendent, but if he's going to retire, we need to bring in someone who will look at the education of our children the same way he does. We don't need to try to fix it. It's fine the way it is."

That man was followed by a woman who wanted to look at philosophical differences. "I agree with the other speaker. We need someone who has the same, or at least similar, philosophy of education as our present superintendent. I think Dr. Smith has a different philosophy of education that would not improve our schools."

The few people who supported Jane made vague remarks that were not always related to education. Their comments might have been more appropriate for a political rally. Most of her supporters, but not all, said that they were from the Cedar Hills area which was where Junior grew up. They saw Jane as being good for the whole county. For example, "I think we need someone who can represent the interests of the county."

One older African-American woman stood out because of the verbal slip she made and the way she jumped up quickly and grabbed the microphone to enthusiastically express her support for Jane.

"I support Dr. Junior Smith for superintendent."

The woman corrected her error, but the reaction in the auditorium was immediate. There was loud laughing and guffawing that reverberated throughout the auditorium. It gave the public some desperately need comic relief that morning. Some people later said they thought the woman had been a plant. They wondered how much Junior had paid her to publicly voice her support for Jane.

On the heels of that, the woman's daughter spoke and said she loved and respected her mother, but she could not, under any circumstances support Jane Smith. The daughter showed courage speaking her mind given the reputation Jane had for retaliation.

My own mother and I talked later about the forum. She concluded that for the people who genuinely wanted someone other than Jane, speaking out had been an exercise in futility. Her opinion was based not only on her experience in education that spanned several decades, but also on her involvement in local politics as a community activist. She firmly believed that the die had already been cast. Jane was going to become superintendent regardless of what the people said at the forum. I still thought that for the board members who listened, the message was clear: The majority of people at the forum did not want Jane as superintendent. I did not understand how the board members could ignore the people who had taken time and made an effort to attend the forum and voice their opinions publicly.

❖

I should have known that Ashley and my mother were right after the visit Louise and I had about three or four weeks before the board meeting when Jane was named as superintendent. It was so unexpected. I was in Louise's office when Phil Carlton, the head of Finance, passed as he headed down the hall to Food Services. Louise called out to him, "Phil! Can you stop back by before you go back upstairs?"

"Why do you want him to come by?" I asked, trying to figure out what she was up to with her request.

"I want to see what he thinks about Jane becoming superintendent. You know Jane and Celeste promised to get rid of him once she became superintendent. They plan to put someone else in his position as head of Financial Services."

I smiled and nodded in agreement. "I know. For some reason Jane just does not like him. He's probably the best person this district has ever had over finances. We were lucky to get him from the state department after he came over for the audit."

"Yes, that was interesting the way he audited the district and the next thing you know, he has a job here in Dane County handling finances for the district." Louise's expression said far more that her words.

I addressed the underlying message in her comment. "There was a lot of talk about it when it happened. We heard that his salary doubled as soon as he signed the contract."

She backed away and didn't take the bait. "It probably did. Those state department employees don't make a lot of money. It's more the status of working for the state department than anything."

"Well he was thrilled to get the job here. I know when Ashley and I went to see him about our contracts he didn't see what the problem was."

Louise raised her eyebrows. "What was going on?"

"Our contract year is for 205 days, but the district only pays 190 days at the doctorate level. That's because the teachers only work 190 days. They drop us back to the Master's level for the remaining 15 days and pay far less."

"I didn't know that. When I was hired, I was given a contract as a consultant. I guess next year they'll pay me the same way." Louise didn't look too pleased at the prospect of having her pay reduced.

"Yes they probably will. Phil told us that we made such good money that he didn't see why we were concerned. Do you know he had the nerve to sit there in Ashley's office and say that to us? And then he said that he was making more money than he had ever made in his life." I was indignant.

"I'm sure he was, if his salary doubled."

By this time we heard Phil coming back down the hall. He walked into Louise's office and sat in the chair by the door, near her desk. "What can I help you with ladies?"

Louise cut to the chase. "Phil we need to know what you think about Jane's bid to become superintendent."

"I think she's going to be our next superintendent."

I reminded him, "There is so much opposition in the county to Dr. Smith. Do you think the board would actually go ahead and name her superintendent in the face of that?"

Phil gave me a patient look, "Yes I do. I think this board is already her board. They are ready to do it today. The only reason they won't do it today is because we still have someone as superintendent. As soon as he retires, Jane will get the position."

The color changed in Louise's face. I could see that she was getting annoyed. She looked directly at Phil and spoke slowly, emphasizing each word. "I think the board has better sense than to go against the people of Dane County."

Phil was unfazed. "All I know is that if you are not on her side, you'd better make amends. That's what I had to do. I went in and had a closed-door conference with her and now we get along just fine. Before that, I'd heard that she was planning to fire me when she became superintendent. I couldn't afford to lose my job. I love living here in Lucien Heights. My wife loves it here and she doesn't want to have to relocate. So I did what I had to do to keep my job."

"She doesn't like us." I tried to explain.

"I know she doesn't. That's why I'm telling you to get on her good side. Find out what the problem is and turn things around."

"I'll never support Jane for superintendent." Louise was adamant.

"I can't support her either. She's not the best person for the job." I had to let him know how I felt.

Phil leaned over closer to us and lowered his voice, "Well I can't force you two ladies to do anything that you don't want to, but I'm giving you the best advice I can. Trust me, you don't want to be on her bad side when she becomes superintendent. I hate to think what could happen."

"What could she do to us?" I asked.

Louise didn't give him a chance to answer my question. She spoke first. "Phil, thanks for your advice, but there's nothing Jane can do to us." She was confident.

When Phil Carlton left Louise's office that day, he had not changed his position and we hadn't changed ours. Louise and I held firm to our position of refusing to support Jane. We didn't think that she could do anything to us that she hadn't already done.

As it turned out, Phil was right.

Ashley was right.

My mother was right.

Louise and I were both wrong.

CHAPTER 3

For the year preceding Jane becoming superintendent, one of our main concerns involved leadership of the Special Services Department. The psychologists had to work closely with a newcomer to the district and to special education, Carlton Lennix.

Mr. Lennix was a capable administrator, but he seemed to be totally out of place directing special education for the county. The district brought him in from one of the coastal counties in the Low Country to head up Special Services even though his only previous administrative experience had been as an elementary school principal. It seems that the assistant superintendent who hired him told him that he only needed to have experience as an administrator … after all, any administrator could handle special education. How naïve.

The parents and teachers all agreed on one thing: Carlton Lennix was a nice man, but he didn't know special education law. It's not that the state and federal regulations were meaningless to him; he simply did not have a special education background.

On one hand, there was that little matter of race with Carlton Lennix. Carlton is a black man. The vast majority of people in the district considered themselves to be sensitive to ethnicity and did not want to be openly critical of him because of his race.

On the other hand, there was the issue of racial pride. A lot of the professional blacks in education were angry that the school district chose someone from out of town with no experience in the field to direct Special Services. They saw it as making all black administrators look bad. Furthermore, they saw it as another example of the district putting a black person in a position to fail and then saying that they attempted to support diversity but it didn't work. They did not understand why the district would do something so patently wrong. They were angry.

Obviously if Carlton Lennix had been white, his qualifications, or lack thereof, would have not been contaminated with the race card. Regardless, I could speak directly to the leadership problems without confusing the issue with race because Carlton and I have race in common. As a black female, I could address the problems concerning his lack of expertise in special education in a way that my white colleagues could not. So I planned to do just that at the first available opportunity.

❖

Call it serendipity.
Call it synchronicity.
Call it providence.

Call it whatever you like, but this is what happened: I saw a tall man with reddish blond hair leaving the building as I got near the main exit after the awards day program at my youngest son's elementary school, Lucien Heights. He looked so familiar. Then I realized that my path had crossed that of one of the school board members, Cooter Wagner, who was leaving the school at the same time that I was. (Everyone knew him by his nickname, Cooter, and rarely called him by his first name, Thomas.) So I went up to him, introduced myself, and started discussing the situation in Special Services. Cooter gave me a quizzical look. He wanted to be certain that he understood everything that I was saying.

He asked me again, "You mean a lot of black people won't get upset if we do something about Mr. Lennix?"

"No, they will not. They will actually be relieved. I'll bet you heard the exact opposite thing from some of the administrators."

He had. The district administrators had convinced the board members that no matter how many problems there were and no matter how many complaints they received, they could not touch Mr. Lennix. It was a sensitive matter.

Now Cooter was hearing from me that everyone wanted something done about the situation, black and white alike, perhaps even Mr. Lennix. He was impressed with this information. His eyes were lighting up, I could see the wheels turning. Cooter was going to do something about it. He told me as much. In fact as he walked off, he said. "Don't worry. The house won't burn down."

I was so excited. I liked Cooter. He always seemed to be a man of integrity. He didn't always call attention to himself, but he had high standards and could be depended upon to give his best in any situation. So I knew help was on the way.

I hurriedly told my colleague when I got back to the office, "Louise, you'll never guess who was at Lucien Heights Elementary this morning! Cooter Wagner! I talked with him about our problems in special education. I think he was truly relieved to know that the district can move Mr. Lennix without offending the black community."

Louise gave me a questioning look. "What was Cooter doing at Lucien Heights Elementary?"

"He has a son who was in the awards program this morning."

"Oh. And Cooter listened?"

"Yes, I'm sure he'd heard about the problems, but I think that he'd been given the impression that nothing could be done about Mr. Lennix to keep from offending the black community."

Louise started laughing, "Thank goodness you were the one who talked with him!" She added, "You know I'm beginning to think that maybe, just maybe, there is light at the end of this tunnel."

We both knew that if Cooter said he would help, he would follow-through and do what he could to help the department and the district.

❖

Now, several weeks after I talked with Cooter and about a month after Louise and I met with Phil Carlton, all of the controversy and the heated board meetings with angry parents had died down and appeared to be a thing of the past. The board acted as if that was all behind them. No more sunrise Saturday morning meetings in the dead of winter with entire families showing up to lodge complaints against Jane. No more little babies sleeping in the mothers' arms while their older siblings tried to stay awake and be quiet as the adults argued desperately to prevent the one woman they felt was most undesirable from becoming the leader of the school system. It was now behind them once and for all … or so it seemed.

Tonight at her inaugural board meeting, Jane Smith was going to be sworn in, and then, from what we'd heard, things could really take off. Jane had her own vision for the school district and was prepared to take whatever steps she had to in her drive to run the district like a corporation. She stressed that the school district was a business … the largest employer in Dane County. People needed to remember that. She was going to get rid of all the administrators who had ever crossed her over the years. She was going to show them all.

Jane would have the power and she would rule.

Celeste Washington called the meeting to order and followed the agenda. Her fellow board members were pumped up and ready to nominate Jane and allow her to begin her reign immediately. Celeste had the honor of swearing Jane in as superintendent. For them, it was probably like a dream come true.

The boardroom was packed. Jane's supporters as well as her detractors were all crowded into the room. People were standing around the wall and pouring out into the hallway on one side and the stairwell on the other. I smiled to myself, someone must have told the fire marshal not to come that night because the numbers clearly exceeded the room's capacity.

The first order of business was for Jane to present her organizational chart. She turned on the overhead projector and the entire room could see what the new organization would look like with her administration. Jane's blonde hair was shining in the light from the projector has she pointed to the various positions on the chart.

My conversation earlier in the evening with John Dye was pushed to the back of my mind allowing me to forget about his prediction about women being upset. I was focused on the meeting. Louise and I had given priority to the Carlton Lennix matter and it was important to see how the board dealt with that. My attention was fully on Jane's new administration and finding out how the director's position would be handled.

After quickly skimming down the positions and names on the chart, I turned to Louise and whispered, "He's still listed as our director. That can't be! They promised to make that change. What do you think happened?"

Louise was furious.

We both felt betrayed.

We had been encouraged by my contact with a board member, Cooter Wagner, a few weeks earlier that the current director of Special Services, Mr. Carlton Lennix, might be removed and placed in another position that would better emphasize his skills.

Just as Louise and I were trying to figure out why that one position had not been changed, we heard Cooter make a comment to Jane. He had to turn slightly and strain a little to look directly at her since the chart was behind him and he had been reviewing something in his board packet on the table in front of him.

"Jane, I think we need to wait until after we meet in executive session before we approve the proposed administration." Cooter probably wondered as we did, why that name was still listed as special education director. He went on to say that he had some questions about positions and strengths. He wanted to be sure that we had the best people in the best positions.

At that point I loved Cooter! He was suddenly my hero. In my mind Cooter was speaking on behalf of all the students in the district, not just special needs, but all of them. I think I saw a small circle of light glowing over his head. A halo? Perhaps. He certainly was an angel in that moment.

Jane didn't seem to understand what he was referring to, but being the experienced politician that she was, she simply agreed that the board had the right to make changes. After all, she knew that her new administration needed board approval. So yes, Mr. Wagner, the chart could be discussed in executive session before the board voted on it.

Later, after the board returned from executive session, Jane Smith announced that there were changes in the organizational chart. She did not go over the positions or state which ones had been changed. There was no further discussion of the chart.

Although Jane did not specifically point it out, one look told us that Mr. Lennix was no longer listed as director of Special Services. Hallelujah!

Our prayers had been answered.

The position was now listed as "Vacant – To Be Filled".

I looked at Louise and she looked at me. We both smiled. We were back on track. Cooter kept his word. He came through for us.

Louise and I were so elated over the prospect of actually hiring a knowledgeable, qualified director of Special Services that we had a mini celebration. After the board meeting that night, we went to the Huddle House for sausage and egg sandwiches with coffee – lots of coffee.

Little did we know. The battle may have been won, but the war raged on at a furious clip.

CHAPTER 4

It was only a few days later we heard the psychologists had been designated as *personae non gratae* by Dr. Smith. Our former supervisor, back when she was assistant superintendent, now wanted us completely out of the administration building, out of the district office.

At last John Dye's prediction made sense. The word was out. We got it from maintenance on two levels, the director and one of the workers. We had to move, but no one knew where we were going. Where would our new offices be located? Would we even have offices?

How could she do this? There wasn't anything on the organizational chart that even hinted at this new development. Why was the board allowing her to do this to us?

We quickly learned that the board was never informed of Jane's plans to kick us out of the district office. Every board member we contacted said the same thing:

They thought the psychologists were going to stay in the district office.

When I called Celeste Washington, the first thing she said was that she didn't know anything about the psychologists being forced to move, but she assumed Jane must have felt that the move would benefit the district. However, if she had an opportunity she would inquire about it. There wasn't anything in what Celeste said that offered real encouragement regarding our situation.

One board member I called started stuttering as he tried to explain what had happened. "She, she … uh, uh, no she didn't say you would have to move. Yes, I guess we could … no, no we didn't uh, uh … approve moving the psychologists."

Pathetic. The man was pathetic.

I reminded the soon to be defeated board member that I had campaigned for him in my precinct, Englewood #1, the largest one in town. It is the only one with a sizable black majority. Every countywide candidate had to carry #1 if they wanted to win.

"I know you supported me. I appreciate it … I appreciate it ... I appreciate all your support. I know you and your family put my cards up downtown … all over your neighborhood." He knew he would never have my support again. The alliance was over, all because he was too cowardly to question the new superintendent … too sorry to speak on our behalf.

Jane controlled the board.

❖

While Louise and I were attempting to get the board to look into the situation, I received a call the following

Monday morning from Dr. Marlena Lyles, the personnel director for the school district. The day before, on Sunday, Marlena had spoken to my mother after church to tell her that the psychologists were no longer going to be allowed to have offices in the administration building. Marlena and my mother were both members of the only black Presbyterian Church in Lucien Heights.

"Claire, did your mother give you my message?" Marlena asked me when she called. "We've decided to move the psychologists out of the administration building."

Marlena went on to explain that I had to move everything out of my office that day or the district would do it for me. But, she was concerned about my personal belongings and wanted me to have a chance to come get them before they were packed up for me by maintenance.

How compassionate. Where was this coming from? Why had I never seen this side of her before? Who was this Marlena? I didn't recognize this 'caring, compassionate' person. Her insincerity was obvious to me, but for whatever reason she seemed to think that it was important to convince me that she cared. Of course I knew better. I knew her too well.

Nevertheless, I still needed more information from her. "Where will our new offices be located?"

"I'm not sure, but I do know that Dr. Smith wants the change completed by the end of the day. She wants the office space for the secretaries. They're going to be moving into the basement area, into the offices that you and the other psychologists currently have."

We had a suite of offices – three psychologists in three adjoining offices with doors that opened to the outside and interior doors that opened to our individual offices. We could close the hall doors and open the doors between the three offices and do consultations or chat or whatever we needed to get done, privately.

Now I was being told that secretaries from upstairs were coming down to the basement and would have the suite.

I felt sadness setting in although the move had not yet taken place. "I'll be there within the next hour."

"Oh, that's great. I won't let anyone touch anything until you get here. I'm in your office now and I'll leave everything just the way you have it." Marlena was effusive in her assurances.

Even though I knew she didn't care what happened to me, I thought that she would at least keep her word about my office. I believed her when she said that I would be able to move my own things.

My two sons, Christian and Michael, were 14 and 10 years old, respectively, that summer when I went to clear out my office. They both volunteered to help me move my things. As can happen with children, in the end only one son went with me, the 14-year-old. That was fine, I thought, because my older son, Christian, would be able to help move the computer and other heavy office equipment.

Christian and I were both somewhat uneasy as we walked downstairs to my office in the basement. We came around the corner at the bottom of the stairwell on the lowest level and headed down the hall to my office. It was obvious that the door was open before we got to the room.

As we started to go into my office, we stopped immediately. Something was wrong … badly wrong.

Where was everything?

Where was the furniture?

My office was empty.

All of my plants were gone – along with the stands.

My personal family photos were gone.

The artwork from students, gifts from children over the years – all gone.

Everything was gone!

There was absolutely nothing left except the phone on the floor near the space where my desk had been.

I cannot begin to describe my feelings at that time. I thought that I was going to pass out.

The empty area did not look like there had ever been an office there.

It was just as if I had never had an office.

My son and I were speechless. We stood there in that emptiness looking from side to side, around the room … then at each other.

What could we say? Marlena had lied.

There was nothing to move. Maintenance had done an outstanding job.

One of the secretaries came in red-faced and apologetic. "Oh Dr. Franklin, I'm so sorry. I didn't know you were coming in. They just told me to pack your things so they could be moved out. I am so sorry!"

I had been annoyed with the board member who began stuttering when he tried to answer my questions about the move, but now it was my turn to stutter … to try to find the words.

"I … uh … I … um … I told Dr. Lyles that I would … um … be here this morning. She knew … She knew that I was coming. Please tell me, where is my office?"

"It's on the truck going to the warehouse. I mean the stuff is boxed up and the boxes are going to the warehouse. I am so sorry. I didn't know. She didn't tell us. She just said to pack up everything so they could send it to the warehouse. I am so sorry."

"She didn't tell you that she spoke with me. She called from this phone … this phone right here on the floor. She called me this morning … at home."

"No, ma'am. She didn't tell us you were coming. She just said pack up everything. I am so sorry."

My son was slowly coming out of the temporary paralysis that resulted from the shock of seeing the utterly empty space where my office had been for so many years. He asked if I was going to talk with Dr. Lyles to find out what happened.

"Yes, I'm going up to her office now. Do you want to come with me?"

No, he said that he thought that he would go out to the car and wait for me.

❖

Walking toward Marlena's office had a surreal quality. I had not been in her office but once or twice before that fateful morning, but we had been friendly and had talked with one another in passing. It was only natural since we were members of the same church and 'sisters' in the same sorority, even though she was closer to my mother's age. When she was hired as the personnel director, I happened to be coming from the parking lot, headed for the D.O. at the same time that she was reporting for work. A mental picture of that meeting stays clear in my mind, even to this day. We stopped on the sidewalk and chatted casually at first, and then our conversation became more pointed. I wanted her to know who could and could not be trusted. As luck would have it, Jane Smith drove up while we were talking. I stressed to Marlena that she needed to be very careful with Jane, who was the assistant superintendent at that time. I explained that Jane had targeted our department and could be a determined woman when she put someone or something on her 'hit list'. I mentioned how the psychologists were constantly under some threat or other from Jane. Marlena nodded that morning as if she understood.

Now I was approaching Marlena's office as I tried to come to terms with the fact that I no longer had an office in the administration building. I was also trying to deal with the fact that my soror, Marlena, had been promoted from Director of Personnel to Assistant Superintendent of Personnel Services when Dr. Jane Smith became superintendent. Times had really changed. Marlena fit right in with Jane's administration. So when I entered her large office area, she immediately turned on the political charm.

"Come on in Claire. Have a seat. I heard about the mix-up and I'm so sorry." Marlena feigned a look of concern.

"I'm still in shock. My office is gone!"

Marlena's voice changed. I noticed that it was devoid of that 'compassionate tone'. She spoke louder as if I were hard of hearing. "There was a mix-up as I said. I suspect that the secretaries were a little over-zealous and they moved you out by mistake."

I stayed calm. I was determined that I would not start arguing with the woman. "But you assured me that my office would not be touched, that I would be able to move my own things out."

"Yes, I thought that you would be able to do that."

"Apparently the secretaries were not told that I would be coming in today to pack up my belongings." I felt I needed to state what had happened from my perspective if for no other reason than to try to make sense of what had turned out to be a cruel hoax.

Marlena waved her hand in the air as if to dismiss the entire situation. "It was just an error. I don't know how the mix-up occurred, but I guess in all the confusion with so much going on around here, mistakes were bound to be made." She looked like her patience was wearing thin.

"Did you talk with the secretaries?"

"I planned to … but … I believe I may have been distracted before I had a chance to speak with them. Don't worry about what went wrong, I'm taking full responsibility for everything that happened."

That last comment was clearly Marlena's way of ending the discussion about my office being cleaned out in my absence. So I moved on to the next logical question that I'd asked earlier, hoping this time to receive an answer.

"Where will my new office be located?"

"We haven't decided."

"We?"

"Dr. Smith and I."

"You haven't decided, but you cleared the offices downstairs?"

"We had to do that because the secretaries were also scheduled to move today. Dr. Smith wants all of this completed by the end of the day."

"I still do not know why the psychologists have to move. Will you please explain why we have to give up our offices."

"One of the consultants hired by the district last month to conduct an efficiency study recommended that the psychologists be placed on itinerant status."

"You hired consultants who made recommendations about the psychologists without meeting with us? Why weren't we given a chance to meet with the consultants? And how can you put us on itinerant status? We don't fall into the same category as itinerant therapists and teachers. They travel between schools and serve the same students throughout the year. We are not itinerant staff!"

"That's subject to interpretation!" Marlena retorted, raising her voice louder.

"Whose interpretation? Why didn't you speak with someone who understands our job description? I think you've been given erroneous information and the recommendation to relocate us is not feasible."

"That's an assumption."

I could tell Marlena was getting angrier, but I felt compelled to continue. "Who better to make it, an outsider who conducted a study of Psychological Services and, for whatever reason, didn't consult the psychologists, but has made some impractical and inappropriate recommendations or a professional who is qualified, certified, and experienced as a school psychologist?"

She pushed her chair back from her desk as if she was getting ready to stand up. "There's nothing that I can do about the move. You might want to consider checking for space in the schools. That would be better than working out of the trunks of your cars."

"Working out of the trunks of our cars?"

"Yes, that has been suggested, but I thought it would be better if you could find a place in the schools rather than to try to do that."

"Who suggested that we could work out of the trunks of our cars?"

"That's not important at this point. I was trying to look out for you and the other psychologists by suggesting the schools. The only person that can undo this is the new

Assistant Superintendent for Instructional Services, Dr. Robert Anderson."

Not only had Marlena helped to do us in, but she was presenting her version of what happened in such a manner that I would be naïve enough to believe that she was actually trying to help us. She and Jane Smith were two of a kind. They were more like sisters than Marlena and I would ever be, sorority or no sorority. Fat lot of good 'sisterhood' did for me.

❖

I later said to my mother, "Mom, it was a waste of time meeting with Marlena. She wouldn't tell me anything other than we needed to meet with the newly hired assistant superintendent, Dr. Robert Anderson. She also said something about it being a shame if we had to work out of the trunks of our cars."

My mother was livid. "Work out of the trunks of your cars? I know she didn't! And she sits her big backside up there in her plush office! Work out of the trunks of your cars. Humph! And all that this family has done for her!"

"You're right. I hadn't thought about it, but you did help her with her position in the church when she moved back to Lucien Heights."

"Yes I did. I didn't share all the information that I had on her with the Presbytery about her past church affiliations. That was so we could allow her to become an elder in our church."

"I asked you back then to be open with the Presbytery. No, you wanted to help out the family because her mother had been so active in the church. But you are

Clerk of the Session and you had a responsibility to let the Presbytery know about her past."

"You're right. But I was trying to help her after she moved back here. You know I have always felt that you don't lose anything by helping someone."

"That's true. But we are dealing with a woman who has a totally different philosophy. She and Jane seem to think alike and now they are using their positions to do dirt together – starting with the psychologists."

When I called Louise that evening, her reaction was very similar to my mother's. After I described how the secretaries were still packing things in the offices and laughing among themselves when my son and I went to my office, Louise decided that she was not going to get involved with the moving. If they wanted her out, the district could do it because she was not going to help them at all.

That's when my friend, Louise, decided to go on vacation. She and her husband left the country. They spent the next week far away from Dane County … in Cancun.

CHAPTER 5

Louise called to tell me what she had planned for us as soon as she returned from her spur of the moment vacation.

"I'm going to make an appointment with Jane. You and I need to meet with her face to face. She's going to have to tell us where the district intends to house us."

Louise had that 'serious as a heart attack' tone and I knew she was right in what she was saying. We did need to meet with Dr. Smith.

The next week as Louise and I sat in the lobby of the D.O waiting to meet with Jane, a man came through the double doors that lead to the first floor offices. He was wearing a shirt and tie minus the jacket. He came through the lobby very quickly – almost too quickly – nearly running upstairs, avoiding eye contact in what appeared to be a deliberate manner.

The man, according to Louise, was Dr. Robert Anderson, Jane's new assistant superintendent. Our future went running upstairs with him and it looked like he wasn't going to deal with it. Louise also said that he knew who we were. He probably did.

When we walked in Jane's office she had a stony expression and made it clear that she had talked with some of the board members. She stated that they had called her soon after we called them. Surprise, surprise.

Jane did not have a clue as to where our offices would be located. She suggested that we call some of the principals to see if they had space in any of the schools. Further, we could get the school secretaries to type the psychological reports. Unbelievable. So much for confidentiality.

It fell on me to say something at that time, so I spoke my thoughts out loud. "Dr. Smith, it really would not work for us to be in the schools. School secretaries have their regular duties without asking them to type reports and take messages for us. And you have to consider that it would be difficult to maintain confidentiality under those conditions."

"That's right, Jane. We need access to the special education records like IEPs and psychological reports. Where will they be housed?" Louise supported my position and pinned Jane down at the same time.

We couldn't be sent to the four corners without access to the records. Jane knew that, but she didn't care. It was no longer her problem. We were no longer under her supervision and besides, she wanted us out of the D.O. Everything else was irrelevant.

At one point Jane left the room to check with her secretary in the office next door. She said she was going to find out when Robert Anderson could meet with us to discuss our office situation. We waited … and waited …

and waited … and then her secretary came in … with a start.

"Oh, you're still here. I didn't hear any talking so I thought you were gone. Where is Dr. Smith?"

Louise replied for both of us, "We thought she was in your office. At least that's where she said she was going … to check Dr. Anderson's schedule."

The secretary was clearly hearing about this for the first time. "No, she didn't come in my office."

"Well where is she?" I asked.

"I don't have a clue."

The secretary then left and was gone for about 5 or 6 minutes before returning. When she came in the second time she made it clear that she couldn't find Jane and then she added with a look of pity, "If it's any consolation, I begged her to leave the psychologists alone. It's not right what happened. But, you know how she is. She wouldn't listen. I'm so sorry things turned out this way." Then she left again.

Finally, after an interminable amount of time, Jane came back. She claimed that she hadn't been able to find the information, but that we should call Dr. Anderson ourselves and schedule an appointment with him. Louise and I never said anything about the secretary looking for her. Somehow it didn't seem appropriate.

❖

We called to schedule an appointment the next day, but it was still more than a week before we could see Dr. Robert Anderson. When Louise and I were finally able to meet with him in his new office on the second floor, he had on an entire suit – unlike the first day we say him sprinting upstairs minus his jacket, avoiding eye contact. The day we met with him, there were still boxes in his office reflecting various stages of unpacking.

Bob Anderson tried to appear ignorant of everything that had happened and took copious notes on the yellow legal pad that would eventually become synonymous with a meeting with him. The truth of the matter was that we knew he was knowledgeable of our situation from our perspective because a good friend of mine was also friendly with his wife. His office manner was typical of most administrators in that he was willing to listen to us, but he made it clear that he had to answer to Dr. Smith, his new supervisor.

Louise was not in a good mood in the meeting and did not want to help make Bob Anderson's job any easier than she had to. She was also unusually reserved. She later said that she knew what an S-O-B he was and she was not going to do his job for him.

In contrast, I felt encouraged in that I assumed that even though Bob Anderson didn't actually offer any options, I thought he would work behind the scenes to help us because my friend had spoken with his wife. When I communicated this to Louise, she admonished me tersely. "He doesn't give a rip about us. He's gonna cover his own ass."

As was often the case, Louise spoke with the accurate voice of experience. She had been, as she put it, behind closed doors many times years ago in the smoke filled rooms with administrators when deals were being cut and careers were being destroyed. You had to respect that. She generally knew what she was talking about when it came to school politics.

When it came to her assessment of Bob Anderson, she was on target. He didn't do anything to help us.

❖

We ended up going to Vo-Teck ... the vocational-technical center for the district. One of the secretaries from the D.O. called to tell me that we would be housed in one of the classrooms at Vo-Teck. The call came almost exactly one week after Louise and I met with Dr. Anderson. When I asked for specifics, she only gave the room number – 733. Said she didn't know anything about the room – or anything about which building it was in – or anything about the size of the room – or anything about anything.

Louise checked it out first. She went with her camera in hand and was stopped by one of the administrators at the entrance of the building where our new offices were located. She told me later that that same administrator at Vo-Teck shouted at her and told her she couldn't take pictures.

"Why didn't he want you to take pictures?"

"He didn't want anyone to see where they are putting us."

"Why not?"

"Because they're putting us in a room that is already occupied."

I was getting a sinking feeling.

"What do you mean already occupied? Who's in the room?"

Louise laughed a cold, hard laugh, "Not just who, but you need to ask what?"

"What? What do you mean – what?"

"There's a take home computer program in the room. The woman that is in charge of the program is just like us. Ha-ha." She laughed that cold, hard laugh again.

"How is she just like us?"

"She's not going to let them get away with what they're doing. They're putting us in on top of her take home computer program. That room is not big enough for all of us!" Louise laughed again after the last comment.

"Well I'm going out to have a look and I'm going to take my camera. Let them try to stop me from taking pictures!"

"Hide the camera until you get in the room. While you're out there, I'm going to the warehouse to see what they've done with our things – our offices."

I decided to take my Polaroid and get shots of the entire room. I couldn't imagine how they planned to move us in a room with another program already in place.

❖

I began to miss having Ashley Howe to talk with at times like this. Ashley had resigned without telling me, after we worked together for so many years. The two of us had seen many other psychologists, male and female, come and go over the years, but we both remained. Then this year all of that changed when Jane Smith kicked us out of the D.O.

I had just walked in the local Roses, when I ran into one of the school nurses.

"Hey Claire. I was sorry to hear about Ashley."

My heart started pounding, "What about Ashley?"

"Oh you know, she decided to leave Dane County so she resigned and got a job in another school district."

"Ashley resigned?"

"Yes. I thought you knew."

The nurse could surely tell by my expression, that the news had a dramatic effect on me. “You didn’t know? Seems like she would have told you first since you two are both psychologists.”

I was truly bewildered. I thought she must have gotten Ashley confused with someone else. Usually there was so much transition at the end of the school year with employees transferring and leaving the district, it would be easy to get one person confused with someone else.

The nurse went on to say that she had talked with Ashley herself and that she was moving to Charleston. Ashley told her that her brother taught in one of the school districts down there so she would be in the same general area that he was in. Ashley had even told her that she and her husband had put their house on the market, but weren’t going to wait for a buyer before moving. They would leave it in the hands of a realtor.

As the nurse told me all of this, I began to feel a little lightheaded, almost as if I would faint. Suddenly I couldn’t remember what I was doing in Roses. It couldn’t have been that important. I felt that I really needed to leave quickly.

So I thanked the nurse and left the store. All the way home, I had the feeling that someone had died. I wanted to call Ashley to ask her what was going on. Why didn’t she tell me that she was leaving Dane County? It didn’t make it any easier for me when I eventually talked with her because I still had to go through the grieving process over the loss of a long-time colleague and, a friend. What she said to me when we talked was that she hadn’t said anything to me because she was afraid that I would have talked her out of leaving. She basically said she was too embarrassed to stay in Dane County after we were booted out of the D.O.

Later that week as I headed to Vo-Teck to take pictures of our new location, I recalled my last conversation with Ashley and how the three of us were now the two of us. It was now Louise and I – just as it had been Ashley and myself off and on for so long. Who would have thought?

❖

It was actually quite easy locating the large room. I saw the same administrator who had given Louise a hard time and I greeted him with a smile. He smiled too and told me how to find the room. He suggested that I let him know if I had any problems or questions. He seemed like a nice man, very helpful.

There was nothing that Louise could have said that would have prepared me for the room with the computers. If I showed someone pictures even now they would not fully understand the magnitude of what had happened.

The room, our new office, had originally been designed for a cosmetology lab. The cosmetology class never got off the ground, which meant that other classes were held in the room until they began using it as the center for the take home computers. So of course all the plumbing fixtures were in place at the rear of the room waiting for the sinks to be used in the cosmetology classes. There was one small office at the front of the large room for Stacy Graves, the take home computer coordinator.

A few days after my initial visit to our new office area at Vo-Teck, Louise called and asked me to come back out to the center. She had the photos from the warehouse and she had arranged for Stacy Graves to be there as well.

Why not? I thought. I wanted to talk with Stacy in her new role as coordinator for the take home computer program. I knew her from her previous role as secretary in one of the elementary schools. She was the person who would get the students from class for me to evaluate. Our conversations were usually limited to the basic pleasantries and thanks from me for helping out. So this would be an opportunity to get to know her in a different capacity.

Stacy had already arrived at Vo-Teck when I got there and was in the room talking with Louise when I walked in. It was obvious from her manner with Louise that the two of them had bonded and were becoming friends. I smiled to myself and thought that Louise moved quickly when circumstances demanded it.

"Hi Louise. Hi Stacy. How are you?"

"I'm ok Claire, and yourself," Stacy answered with a pleasant smile.

"I'm fine. Louise told me that you are like the two of us. You also have a problem with this arrangement."

"Yes, I do have a problem with it. I don't see how it's going to work."

"What do you think we need to do?" I wanted to know if she was aware of some options that Louise and I had not considered.

"We need to talk with the director of Vo-Teck and ask him if he can't find another area for your offices."

Louise responded that she hoped Stacy would have better luck than she had with the director. He basically told her that this was the best they could do and he wasn't going to take space from any of his vocational classes to give district office staff new offices. The district had a responsibility to provide office space for us. He thought that allowing us to share the room with Stacy was a generous move on his part and he could not and would not do anything more.

Stacy simply said, "We'll see," and then left to look for the director.

❖

While we waited for Stacy to get back from talking with the director, Louise reminded me of the other reason for my visit to Vo-Teck that afternoon. "I have three sets of pictures from the warehouse. One for you, one for me, and one set 'just in case'." She then handed me my set of photos and waited for my reaction.

It looks like they just tossed our things in on top of equipment, old furniture, anything that was in the warehouse.

"I wanted you to see it for yourself, without my having to describe it for you".

"Clearly there was no respect of personal property… just boxes with labels on them and odd shaped items unmarked lying on top."

It was all very disheartening.

"Look at the records. The file cabinets are not secured, they don't even have locks."

"How could they do that with highly confidential special education records and psychologicals?"

"Claire, they don't care."

"That's obvious."

"Al told me to tell you that we should write about this one day and tell the world about this and what they did to the flag."

Al was Louise's husband, but I didn't understand what he was referring to by mentioning the flag. "Louise, I'm not sure I follow you."

"Look at the pictures again and look for the American flag."

I did just that. I looked through the photos again and I noticed that at least three of them had a flag in them."

"Do you see where the flag is?"

"Yes, it's on the floor … and it looks dirty."

"That's what upset Al. The school district had allowed the flag to be treated in that manner."

"Oh, I believe I read somewhere once that there is a proper way to dispose of a flag when it's no longer going to be used."

"Oh yeah, there is. I'll be honest with you, that whole scene up at the warehouse really got to both of us, but Al had a hard time dealing with the way the district disrespected the American flag. Claire, it was on the floor and it was clear that people had been walking over it and it was filthy."

"How awful."

"Al was beside himself! He reminded me that men lost their lives fighting for that flag. He fought in World War II and the Korean War. It's just hard for a person who has been in the military to understand how they could let something like that happen."

I reminded her, "It's what you said before. They just don't care."

CHAPTER 6

Stacy had said, "We'll see," as she left to go find the director. Well, we did see and it didn't take long. The next day all of our furniture and boxes were delivered to the big room at Vo-Teck, room 733.

It was one grand and glorious mess.

Stuff was all over the place.

The furniture looked as if it had been thrown haphazardly in the room – still with our names on masking tape labels.

Boxes of all sizes were strewn about.

If maintenance didn't appear to care at the warehouse, they sure as heck didn't care in room 733.

Louise said it was a picture that she would take with her to her grave.

We called the D.O. and talked with Dr. Anderson.

We called the center director again.

We called board members.

We called Jane Smith.

We called everyone and anyone we could think of who might possibly do something to help us. It was all a waste of time – the calling.

By the time the calling ended, it was time to go back to work. The school year was beginning and we had lost a summer trying to find a place for our offices.

❖

Dr. Bob Anderson came to Vo-Teck with what he said was great news on our first day of the new school year. The man strutted into room 733 with a smile on his face. He had figured out a way to give us each our own individual office and solve the privacy problems – all in one fell swoop. He had placed a special order that morning before coming out to Vo-Teck. He was going to bring in partitions – acoustic partitions.

"Don't you think that's great?" He was so ebullient. He said he remembered them from the State Department of Education in Columbia when he worked there and figured they would be the perfect solution to our dilemma.

We would have our very own cubicles, thanks to the partitions. Dr. Anderson said he was aware that we had private offices before, but we needed to be team players and cooperate. After all, we shouldn't fight change. We should embrace it. These partitions would give us privacy and the feel of an office without the expense of the district having to build new offices. "Now ladies, I don't want to hear any objections".

He then turned to me, "Oh, by the way Claire, we think that your table from the D.O. is too large to fit in the partitioned office. Would you like to donate it to the D.O.?"

Was I hearing him correctly? They had the unmitigated gall to evict us on short to no-notice without anyplace to go, toss us on the street and now he wanted to keep my table?

"Dr. Anderson, I appreciate your concern but I'd like to have all of my office furniture here at Vo-Teck. The table is a part of my office and I still need it."

His expression changed. "Well if you want to keep it that's fine. I was only trying to help. I'll have maintenance deliver it before the end of the week."

When he left Louise commented that they were so dirty trying to hold on to my table because it was a nice piece of solid furniture, not the regular flimsy tables in the other offices at the D.O.

I thought about it and realized that she was right. My table was old-fashioned with large drawers and nice handles. It was an exchange from the former maintenance director for the district when they moved us to the basement. He offered me a great wooden table in exchange for the mostly metal one I had upstairs in my office. I quickly accepted the offer; I knew was getting the best part of the deal. So yes, the table stayed with me. And no, heck no, it was not going to the district office. No way.

❖

Louise came into room 733 excited several days later. She had called Fred Hines on the school board. The two of them had been friends for years, ever since back when he had been principal at Lucien Heights Middle School and she was directing special education … a previous lifetime for them both.

Louise announced that Fred was coming to Vo-Teck to check on our office area in room 733. Fortunately when Fred arrived, the partitions were in place and he could see the best that the district had to offer us.

"Hey Fred, come on in." I could hear Louise greet Fred Hines as he entered room 733 for the grand tour. I had just received a call from a parent so I couldn't speak to him at that point. As I talked on the phone I could hear the voices of Louise and Stacy in the background talking with Fred.

By the time I finished the phone call Fred Hines was gone. Stacy and Louise were dancing around the room, grinning from ear to ear. I assumed that they were both very pleased about what had happened while Fred was there.

Louise confirmed it, "Claire, you missed it. Fred is furious!"

Louise continued by describing how Fred left room 733 terribly upset and had gone through the entire building to see if there was any office space available. "He found two offices that he said we should be able to use. He said he's going straight to Jane's office and she is going to have to free up those offices for us! He could hear you on the phone with that parent and he said this is disgraceful … to put professionals in these cubicles with no privacy. He said we are going to get offices!"

How fortuitous.

We found out later that Fred was especially angry because Jane had given all of the secretaries at the D.O. their own private offices to keep from having enough space to bring us back. The secretaries had private offices and the psychologists were in cubicles. He was livid.

The next week the sun was shining brightly. The director of Vo-Teck suddenly realized that there were two offices that we could have.

Stacy was thrilled. We were leaving room 733 and she could reclaim her space.

We were thrilled as well. We were leaving room 733 and Stacy could reclaim her space. We each now had private offices. Life was good.

❖

In spite of all the office wrangling that surrounded us, Louise and I were also trying to deal with the school assignments. Jane Smith decided not to hire any more psychologists. We had always been understaffed, even when Ashley was with us, but now we had to serve 17 schools between the two of us. The very idea that two psychologists would have to provide a full array of services for that many schools in the district was unconscionable.

Louise and I decided to eliminate Vo-Teck from the 17 schools since students came there from the four county high schools. It did not have its own student population, per se. That still left 16 schools for us, but we could at least divide those 16 schools evenly with eight each. There wasn't any way to divide the county equally and we ended up with our eight schools being in different parts of the county. Even with that there were too many schools per psychologist. There was no way that only two people could provide ongoing, quality psychological services to all of those schools.

We spoke with Dr. Anderson to try to get him to advocate for hiring another psychologist, but he said it was out of his hands. Dr. Smith was the only one who could authorize filling the vacant position. Jane Smith refused to discuss the matter with us. When Louise and I decided to ask Fred Hines to question her about the vacant position, Jane sent us a message that she would get rid of us and do contract testing, if we didn't stop trying to pressure her into hiring another psychologist. Well that was absurd in my opinion. So I sent a message back – by the same board member – that the community would never allow her to get rid of the full-time psychologists and contract for evaluations. Our jobs involved much more than testing.

Who would handle the consultations?

Who would handle the staffings?

Who would handle the classroom observations?

Who would handle all the other duties that we had as psychologists?

And, what about the records? Louise and I both had stressed the need to have appropriate, professional access to the special education records on an ongoing basis. It was the difference between having to go to the administration building to access the records versus having the records available at Vo-Teck. We had never been without the records. When we were moved from the second floor at the D.O. to the basement, we had access to all of the current records. The main records remained upstairs on the second floor, but all we had to do was go up two flights of stairs to access them. Now we had to go 10 miles – five miles each way – from Vo-Teck to the administration building to see records. That became problematic if, for example, one of us discovered that we needed to review records on a child after we had already been to the D.O. once – or twice – that day.

Access to the records and the availability of records had to be given priority. Louise and I scheduled another meeting with Dr. Bob Anderson to consider options for making the records more accessible. He opened the meeting with an answer to the continuing unspoken question, “Dr. Smith wanted me to convey to you two ladies her sincere desire to make the records more accessible and she wanted me to be certain that you understood that moving the psychologists back to this building is not an option”.

Louise responded, “Thank you for giving us that message from Jane. You can take one back to her. We did not come here today to ask to be moved back to this building. If she wants to make the records more accessible, she can move them to Vo-Teck with us.”

“Oh no, we can’t do that,” Dr. Anderson replied with the sound of anxiety in his voice. “I talked with Dr. Smith at length about sending the records out to the vocational center. She said that we needed to leave them here because the new director said she wants them to remain in this building so that her secretary will have daily access to them.”

“Let me get this straight. Dr. Smith wants to keep the records in this building for a secretary? We’re the professionals and we are the ones whose job depends on access to those records. Doesn’t Jane understand that?” Louise was irritated.

Dr. Anderson tried to assuage her concerns, “I think she understands that. In fact, I know she does because I’ve come up with what I think is the perfect solution to the records question.”

I looked at Louise and she looked at me. It was never a good thing when Dr. Anderson came up with a solution that he saw as perfect. Those acoustic partitions were more than enough proof of that.

I asked, "Dr. Anderson, it's wonderful that you have solved our dilemma. What is your 'perfect' solution?"

He was brief and to the point. "We're going to copy the records."

"Copy the records?" Louise and I asked the same question at the same time.

"Yes," he said looking back and forth between the two of us with a smile.

I needed to be certain that I heard correctly, "All of them?"

"Why of course. It wouldn't do to send you some of the records and not send them all to you."

"That's over a thousand records." Louise wanted to be sure that he understood the magnitude of his 'solution'.

"Oh, I know. But, don't worry. We've already begun copying and as soon as the copies are ready, they're going to be sent to Vo-Teck."

"Oh my." I was at a loss for words.

Louise was not. "That's an ambitious undertaking." By the tone in her voice, I could tell she had passed being irritated and was now getting angry.

"It is. But, we're giving it our best shot. After all, what choice do we have?"

"None, I guess." I said that, but I was unconvinced.

Dr. Anderson was so proud of his role in resolving the records issue, that he asked the perfunctory, "Is there anything else that I can help you with?"

He probably should not have asked, but since he did, I had a request for him. "What is going to be done about secretarial services for us at Vo-Teck?"

"The Special Services secretary can't handle our reports and correspondence if she is at the district office and we're at Vo-Teck." Louise wanted to get as much out in the open as possible.

Not to be outdone, since he had solved the records problem, Dr. Anderson said, "Let me get back with you on that. I need to get approval from Dr. Smith if we're going to hire someone to type reports and handle your correspondence."

"We'd really appreciate that," I said.

"Do you have someone in mind?" he asked.

"Why not hire the same woman who did our typing when we were in the basement."

"Oh, ok. I'll give her name to Dr. Smith. Is that everything?"

"Yes," I replied. "Thank you so much for your assistance with all of this."

He shook our hands, "You're welcome. I'll call as soon as I have answer from Dr. Smith regarding a typist."

When he was out of earshot Louise asked me, "Can you believe that he's going to all of that trouble? They're copying all of the special education records … just for me and thee?"

"He probably doesn't have a choice. They'll do anything to keep us out of the D.O. It's such a shame."

"Think about how much it's going to cost them in time and effort – not to mention paper and folders."

I laughed and observed, "Cost is not a factor."

"What they don't realize is that they're making themselves look bad. Now they're having to basically put together another department at Vo-Teck."

"It's like a dream come true … a Department of Psychological Services."

"Uh-huh. With a staff of two psychologists." Louise had a way of staying grounded in reality.

"But the fact of the matter is that we're not going backwards. We're still going forward. We're making progress." I was determined to remain optimistic and positive.

Louise conceded, "That's true. Fred Hines got us private offices and now Bob Anderson is copying records and talking about hiring a typist for us."

"Oh, and don't forget the phones."

"I can't leave the phones out."

When we were given our individual offices, Dr. Anderson arranged for us to get two private phone lines. We had two phones with two lines and each phone had an answering machine.

I laughed again, "Not bad for two people that Jane wanted to work out of the trunks of their cars."

CHAPTER 7

In my mind Jane was crazy with power. I later learned that my opinion was shared by the majority of professionals in the district.

Things were happening so quickly. Jane was making changes almost on a daily basis. There was a difference in the atmosphere in the schools that was almost imperceptible at first, but it became very pronounced in a few months.

According to the school district rumor mill, Jane and Marlena were creating a reign of terror. People were being fired without cause and for the slightest thing.

Paranoia became the norm.

Teachers were afraid to talk with their colleagues in the teachers' lounges throughout the district. As everyone knows, teachers' lounges are notorious for information you can access just by sitting in them and listening to conversations. Well now there were fewer conversations and few – hardly any – teachers going to the lounges, except to use the restrooms. Everyone felt that everyone else was a spy for Jane. No one trusted anyone. Long time friends were suddenly suspicious of one another. Teachers as well as some administrators thought that everything they said would get back to Jane eventually and she would act vindictively.

Freedom of speech was guaranteed in the U. S. constitution, but not in Dane County School District.

There was a popular joke going around during that time: What is the difference between Jane Smith and God? The answer was that God knew he wasn't Jane Smith.

❖

By November of that year, Jane's first year as superintendent, I started to have some minor health problems. However, it wasn't until near Thanksgiving that I realized I might actually have a serious medical condition. I became so sick that I was rushed 45 miles away to a hospital emergency room in Columbia in the middle of the night. It was then that the medical tests revealed that my gall bladder was the culprit. The physicians in the ER recommended immediate hospitalization. My hospital stay lasted approximately two weeks.

I'm not sure if it was because I was in Columbia and not Lucien Heights, but Junior Smith – that's right Jane's husband, Junior – came by the hospital to see me. Junior and I had always worked well together when he was a principal, but even so, I thought it was a bit unusual for him to come out of town, all the way to Columbia, just to check on me. I appreciated the visit, but I was extremely ill and don't recall much other than he said he heard I was in the hospital and he wanted to let me know that he and Jane were thinking about me.

Many people have suggested there was a less altruistic reason for the visit. People tended to believe that nothing was ever as it seemed when it came to Junior and Jane. They assumed that whatever they did would benefit one or both of them in some way. I don't know.

Following my initial hospital stay, I was able to return to work briefly, but I couldn't stay long because I had to have gall bladder surgery after Christmas.

When I was hospitalized the second time for surgery, both Junior and Jane came to see me. That was totally unexpected – the Smiths coming by to visit me in Columbia. Both of them were smiling and Jane brought me a book, *Meditations for Women Who Do Too Much.* She said she suspected that my health problems were related to job stress. I thought that people were wrong in saying that Jane wasn't smart. She figured that out.

CHAPTER 8

Call it serendipity.

Call it synchronicity.

Call it providence.

Call it whatever you like, but this is what happened: I ended up being out for eight weeks in the spring of that school year just as all hell broke loose in the district.

As fate would have it, while I was out on medical leave, Jane decided to move one of the most popular high school principals in the county, Monty Ray Hill, from his school in the Riverplains area to the district office. Jane reassigned him to supervise the Department of Buildings and Grounds for the school district. Unlike previous superintendents, Jane did not have to have a reason, she ruled by fiat. The rumor was that she was angry with Monty Ray and wanted to punish him. We never found out the truth of the matter, because like everything else involving Jane, the truth was elusive.

I learned about Jane moving Monty Ray during a phone conversation with Stacy. She called me at home to discuss a newly formed parent group, PUBS – Parents United for Better Schools – which she was closely involved with. As we talked, she explained what Jane had done with Monty Ray and let me know that there was an uprising countywide. The momentum was building.

My response underscored my skepticism. "The parents are getting organized in Dane County? That is amazing! This has always been the most do-nothing, apathetic area of the state."

I couldn't understand how things had changed so dramatically in just a few months. People were now forming groups in opposition to Jane? This was wonderful news, but I remained incredulous.

Stacy and I talked for quite a while and she explained that the students and parents in the Riverplains area of the county were angry with Jane for moving Monty Ray, especially at this time of the school year when they still had to have the prom and graduation. The seniors wanted Monty Ray to give them their diplomas. The students loved him. In their minds he was still their principal.

Stacy told me that one of the seniors, Gregory Townsend, was taking the leadership role for the community. Greg was going to get the residents of Riverplains to demand that Monty Ray be returned to the high school. It was quite a challenging enterprise for such a young man, but Greg was determined to get Monty Ray back.

After Stacy and I talked, I tried to figure out why the county would be mobilizing now against Jane when this was not the worst thing that she had done. I concluded that it was because she had evidently made a very poor decision by moving someone as popular as Monty Ray in the first place and then secondly, in moving him from Riverplains High at this point in the year.

Monty Ray gave new meaning to the word 'popular'. It was said that the majority of the students loved him. Even the girls felt comfortable going to him with their problems and had no hesitation in asking him for advice. He was apparently extremely well respected in Riverplains.

❖

What did this mean? If the county residents were beginning to wake up and take notice of what Jane was doing, did this mean that we might be able to do something about her as our superintendent? Did this mean that the psychologists might be able to move back to the district office with our records and Special Services?

Suddenly so many things were beginning to look like real possibilities.

It didn't take long though, for everyone to realize that Dr. Jane Smith had no intention of admitting that she had made a mistake and she certainly was not thinking about resigning as superintendent.

Louise stressed that Jane would never resign and the only way to get rid of her would be for the board to fire her. But, these were the same nine people who had unanimously named her superintendent. They were not going to admit that they had made a mistake when they had given her their total unswerving support in the face of so much opposition even before she had been named superintendent. No, this board was not about to deal with Jane.

Stacy, Louise, and I talked about the possibility of getting some of the board members to vote against Jane. It was not going to happen. Besides, we needed at least five votes, a majority of the board members, to support any action against Jane. We knew that the chances of that happening were slim to none.

But, as the three of us tossed our options around, one of us mentioned a new board. "Yeah, that's it. We need a new board."

The problem was that the board seats came up for reelection every two years, alternating even and odd numbered seats. So if we could find individuals willing to run for the board, the most we could elect that year would be four. And that was assuming that our candidates could defeat the incumbents. That was normally difficult, defeating incumbents. We would have to have 100% success. Even with that we still would need one more vote to take action against Jane.

We needed a new board that would listen to the constituents, the voters, the county residents. The one good thing was that there was no longer a silent majority in our county. The majority of voters in Dane County were anything but silent now. They were highly vocal and outspoken at every opportunity.

The protests grew larger at each board meeting. I heard that at one board meeting there were over a thousand people present. I wanted desperately to go, but I was still out on medical leave and I knew that Jane would use that against me the way she used it against another psychologist a few years earlier. The woman had been out following back surgery, but was able to go to a bowl game in Florida, with her doctor's permission. She had the unfortunate luck of running into Jane and her husband, Junior, at the game. Jane saw the woman only one more time after the bowl game … to ask for her resignation. She got it. Ashley and I finished the year out as the only two full-time psychologists. Louise was then hired later as a contract psychologist.

❖

By now the news media had picked up the story about the ongoing protests and Dane County School District was once again in the state news. Ah … It was almost like old times, except this time it was much more powerful.

The first time we made state level news was less than a year earlier at the beginning stages of Jane's administration following the change to shared principals at four rural elementary schools. The vote to change to 'Share-A-Principal' was allegedly held in executive session, which is a violation of Freedom of Information (FOI). The parents of the four schools involved tried to get the board to rescind the vote, but the board refused to reconsider it.

Therefore, the parents of the schools with the shared principals took their case public. They contacted the TV stations in Columbia and gave interviews explaining why they opposed the concept of shared principals. For some reason, Jane had only done this at four rural schools. She didn't do it necessarily at the smallest ones; it made no sense. It seemed vindictive which was in keeping with the way Jane made decisions.

One of the parents, Vicky Temple, decided to bring suit against the school district for FOI violations. She retained a prominent attorney from Columbia who was very knowledgeable about FOI. The lawsuit alleged a flagrant violation of FOI and charged that a vote was taken in executive session over the change to shared principals for four schools. Vicky had the support of a small cadre of parents from one of the shared principal schools and these parents were determined to advocate on behalf of their children for as long as it took.

There was some mystery about Vicky Temple and the lawsuit. No one really knew where the money was coming from for her to be able to retain a high-powered attorney from Columbia. It was suspected that she must have had financial backing from a private source, someone who wished to remain anonymous. The answers were never revealed because the lawsuit never made it to court.

Louise called me one evening during the holiday period before my gall bladder surgery to tell me of the horrible news she had just received.

"Do you remember Vicky Temple?"

"Who?"

"You know, Vicky Temple, the woman who was suing Jane over FOI violations."

"Oh, yeah. What about her?"

"She's dead."

Was I hearing her correctly? "Dead?"

"Yes, she died tonight."

I did hear her correctly. Oh, my God. "How? What happened?"

"The story is that she was out selling cosmetics, visiting customers, and her car went out of control on a rain soaked secondary road out in the county."

It was true the weather had been bad with a lot of rain. It was not hard to imagine that the roads might have been slick, dangerously slick.

"Some man happened to be behind her and he saw the whole thing. Said her car skidded into a tree and burst into flames. He pulled her from the car before her body could be burned. The car was totally destroyed."

"How horrible. That is so tragic. Have you heard anything about her family?"

"Just that her husband said she should have left Jane alone."

"You don't think … does he think this had something to do with the lawsuit?"

"I don't know. I'm just repeating what I heard. Who knows? He probably is so overcome with grief, he's not aware of what he's saying. They had two young children."

We heard later that Jane Smith was at a party at the home of one of the board members during the Christmas holidays. The party was a gift products show and sale for Christmas items. Jane reportedly laughed out loud and told someone at the party that she felt great now that she no longer had the lawsuit to worry about. Then she said with a gigantic smile that her problems were all over.

Louise told me that story. She also told me that the parents of the shared principal schools who had been granting interviews to the press in opposition to the plan were now eerily silent. You had to wonder.

CHAPTER 9

There were complaints about Dr. Jane Smith and her administration from one end of Dane County to the other and from one side of the Sandhills River to the other. People were angry with Marlena Lyles for doing Jane's dirty work. As head of personnel for the district, she had managed to become the acting 'hatchet man' for Jane. So many people fell prey to the duo, Jane and Marlena.

One glaring example of this was the assistant principal at Lucien Heights Elementary who was well liked by the teachers and the community. As is customary in schools, because she was an assistant principal, she was given primary responsibility for disciplining the students. The woman quickly established herself as fair and even handed with disciplinary matters. The teachers, students, and parents learned early on, after she became an administrator, that she did not play favorites. Students were disciplined according to the rules, without exceptions. She was frequently left in charge of the school when the principal was out for allergies ... or sinus problems... or a virus ... or the bug du jour. At those times she ran the school efficiently and was generally found to be a good administrator. If she had a flaw it was that she was too trusting. She decided to apply for a position as a principal in one of the other elementary schools and went to talk with Dr. Marlena Lyles about her aspirations. Marlena told her that she would have to resign from her current position as assistant principal, that is, effectively resign from the district, and then apply for the position of principal in the other elementary school. The woman trusted Marlena and resigned. Of course she ended up without a job near the opening of the next school year.

When I learned about the assistant principal's plight, I questioned where was her basic survival instinct in that situation. No one had ever had to resign from their job in the school district in order to apply for another position within the district. That was absurd. Marlena knew better. The assistant principal should have known better. You didn't have to be rocket scientist to figure that one out. There were several people applying for other administrative positions within the district during that time and no one else was told they had to resign.

The fact that this woman was without a job in the weeks before school opened that year troubled me greatly. I felt that someone needed to intervene on her behalf, so I paid Celeste Washington a visit. Sometimes I called Celeste, but for that one I needed to do a face to face. I was relieved to learn that Celeste was aware of the situation and had already told Jane to find the woman a job. Celeste was too much of a professional to say anything negative about Jane or Marlena, but she told me enough for me to know that she didn't give either of those ladies any wiggle room.

They had to rehire her for an administrative position at once. She called me the next week to let me know that the woman was being given a part-time teaching and part-time administrative position in the Cedar Hills area near her home. Celeste had intervened and an employment disaster was averted. I am convinced that the woman would have been seeking employment in another school district if Celeste had not gotten involved.

❖

One guidance counselor at Lucien Heights High School, our flagship school, got called into her principal's office first thing in the morning. He told her she needed to pack her things because Dr. Lyles had called and said she could no longer stay at school. Her certification was not in order. The woman was mortified.

The counselor thought that the certification questions had been resolved after her last conference with Marlena. At that meeting Marlena told her to take the next national area exam for guidance and that everything would be all right. She assured the counselor that her permit from the State Department of Education would be continued for another year.

The counselor felt that she had been misled by Marlena. Her principal would not answer any questions. He simply told her that he was following a directive from the personnel office.

The principal claimed he no choice. He had to follow orders which meant that, no, she could not finish the day out. He was sorry if she had appointments scheduled for the afternoon. The parents would have to understand. She couldn't be expected to keep the appointments if she was no longer a district employee. He reiterated, the parents would have to understand.

The counselor did not feel that she could make any sense out of what the principal was saying, so she called Dr. Lyles to find out what personnel wanted her to do. Marlena was not available. Imagine that. But her secretary told her that she had to leave the premises immediately. No, the secretary did not have any more information than that. She had to leave at once. Oh, following repeated questioning, the secretary remembered one important bit of information. The board voted last night to ask her to leave first thing in the morning. That's why they called the principal so that he could handle it on that level. She was so sorry, but Dr. Lyles was gone for the day. Perhaps the counselor could call next week and schedule an appointment. No, she really didn't want to try to schedule a meeting without Dr. Lyles being here to tell her how long the meeting would take and who else needed to be included. So sorry. Please call next week.

The counselor packed her belongings in a daze. She reflected on the experience later and wondered how she had maintained her sanity and professionalism as she left school. Just like that. It was all over. She left home that morning with a job and came home an hour later without a job. It was a nightmare. But she did make the call the next week – to an attorney. She thought that she would find out what her rights were, if any.

❖

There were many similar stories in Dane County over the course of Jane's first year as superintendent. Some people were too embarrassed to talk about what happened to them. Others were only too happy to find a sympathetic ear or two.

As with any situation, Jane had her defenders. They were considerably fewer in numbers, but they supported her nevertheless. She had the majority of district office secretaries on her side. Thanks to her each one of them acquired huge offices all to themselves just like the administrators. It was great for them to be able to decorate their new offices and compare décor from room to room.

Jane also had support from the Finance Department, newly moved to the basement and from the Food Services Department, which remained in the basement. She managed to get the support from these two departments because she had the district completely remodel an area in the lower level that was previously used by the nurses. Whenever the subject of remodeling had come up with prior superintendents, the main objection was that the nurses' room had to remain intact because they needed the sinks. Jane took care of that objection by sending them out into the schools. That way they couldn't possibly need the sinks if they were no longer in the building to use them. Each nurse was forced to find a school to call her home base and the room at the D.O. in the basement soon became a distant memory. After the renovations, the room faded from memory completely. It had become nonexistent.

Louise and I had gone by the D.O. during the remodeling and we had to carefully negotiate our way through the basement area around construction materials and workers in order to access our former offices. It turned out that the secretary we needed to speak with was in my old office. She said that they had begged to be allowed to stay upstairs on the first floor in their former offices, but that they were told that those offices had already been assigned to another department. The secretary seemed so unhappy over the turn of events.

Just as Louise and I were leaving the Finance Department, we ran into Fred Hines, who had been instrumental in securing decent offices for us at Vo-Teck. We stopped to speak and Louise said to him, "We still don't know why they moved us out."

He asked her, "What did Jane say about it?"

"We've heard about four or five different versions of what happened. If Jane has a valid reason, she hasn't bothered to share it with anyone that we've talked with."

Fred shrugged his shoulders, seemingly unconcerned. "You've got nice offices at Vo-Teck now. At least you're not in the basement."

Louise replied, "No, we're not in the basement, but we're not at the D.O. either. We're district level personnel, we shouldn't be at Vo-Teck, we're supposed to be here in this building."

Fred clearly didn't want to discuss it any further. "I'd leave it alone if I were you. Trust me, you're much better off out of this building." Having said that, he turned and headed down to one of the construction workers, effectively ending the conversation.

Louise didn't say anything else. There was no need to. We got the message.

❖

Dr. Jane Smith as superintendent was turning out to be far worse than anyone could have imagined. I thought that I had heard everything until Louise called me to tell me the latest that Jane had done.

"Claire, are you sitting down?"

"Louise, you know I hate it when you ask me that. What has Jane done now?"

"I want you seated when you hear this so you can jump and scream."

"That bad, huh?"

"Worse."

"Ok. I'm sitting down."

"Jane gave back over $400,000 of school district money."

"What! Who did she give it back to … the state department?"

"No, the county – the county council."

"How could she do that and why would she do something like that?"

"The way I understand it is that she claims to have saved the county nearly half a million dollars and she returned the money."

By this time, my voice was beginning to sound shrill. "You can't give school district money back to the county or the state or the federal government!"

"Apparently you can. Jane did." Louise's tone was still flat, but her words were drawn out in her sometimes slow, deliberate style so I knew she did not like what had happened.

"No," I insisted. "You spend it because if you don't, you'll get less the next time. That's the way that works."

"I know, but Jane didn't play by the rules. She made up her own – to give money back."

"How did she get away with that?"

"That spineless bunch of rubber stampers will allow her to do whatever she wants to do … with their blessing."

"That's terrible! How can anyone take money away from a school district and give it to the county council?"

"Jane can and did. It's a done deal."

"Oh my God! She took money from the children!" My voice was quite high-pitched by now. "Jane knows how hard it is to get money for education – for schools. Why would she do something like that?"

"To look good for the county council. There are some of us who believe that that was a part of the deal she cut to become superintendent."

"What do you mean?"

"Well, by promising to give money back, she had support from unlikely quarters. You know the county council is controlled by the Republicans."

"So she had Republican support because of the money?"

"Sure, that's how she got voted in by the board even though the people of Dane County made it clear they did not want her as their superintendent of schools."

"But where would the half a million come from? It's not as if we have hundreds of thousands of dollars lying around waiting for Jane to give away to the county."

"No, but think about all the positions that she has eliminated this year so far."

That made absolutely no sense to me. "Salaries? She found over $400,000 in salaries to give away? How?"

"Easy. If she eliminated 10 jobs that paid $40,000 each, that's your $400,000 right there. But, she didn't have to do it that way. She could fire five or six custodians and cafeteria workers and then eliminate two principals the way she did with the shared principals and that would add up."

"But not to nearly half a million in those salaries. Custodians don't make $40,000."

"They don't have to ... It costs the district roughly twice the salary for each full-time employee."

"What on earth are you talking about?"

"Benefits. Let's use a principal as an example. If the principal's salary is $65,000 per year, the school district – as the employer – sometimes has to pay nearly an equal amount into retirement, social security, and health insurance for that person."

"Oh, so if a principal makes $65,000 a year, it can actually cost the district as much as $130,000?"

"That's exactly right."

"I had no idea."

"Most people don't know that, but that's a part of school finances."

"And Jane eliminated enough positions and fired enough people to get the half a million?"

"She may not have had to fire that many people … just not fill some vacant positions … like Ashley's position."

"Oh, no!"

"Oh, yes."

"This woman is really an abomination. No wonder people hate her."

"Now we see why so many people fought so hard to keep her from becoming superintendent."

"They didn't know she would do something like this, did they? I mean, how could they?"

"Probably not. But, they did know that she would allow the politically powerful to be more involved in school district affairs than they needed to be."

"Do you think this will make the news?"

"I doubt it. It's not the kind of thing they'd want the public to know." And then she added sarcastically, "The superintendent took money from the school children and gave it to the county to make herself look good … as a businesswoman."

In spite of what Louise and I thought, or anyone else for that matter, Jane never looked back and she never slowed down. Her supporters were thrilled. They felt that she was finally doing something about what they perceived as 'problems' in the school district. Her detractors were horrified. They felt the woman had to be stopped. As the days and weeks passed, the detractors and critics became increasingly vocal and grew in number.

CHAPTER 10

Suddenly Dane County was big news again. This time Monty Ray's reassignment and Greg Townsend's rallies were feeding the media.

PUBS made the news too. Initially the members were from the Riverplains area, but now they represented every area of the county. There were even T-shirts with "I survived Dr. Jane Smith" on the front and a list of things that Jane had done on the back with a box by each item on the list and a checkmark in each box. An enterprising businessman in the Riverplains area had come up with the idea of T-shirts and was doing quite a brisk business. We were told that he couldn't keep them in stock they were selling so fast. It seems that half the county wanted to wear the T-shirt.

The situation with Monty Ray was taking on a life of its own. He was becoming something of a local celebrity. The students were meeting on a daily basis. They wanted their voices to be heard loud and clear. As the small rallies became large rallies, the news media started giving major coverage to the goings on in Dane County. The area was becoming the topic of discussions all over the state.

Then one morning everyone opened their *Carolina* newspaper, a statewide daily, and guess who was on the front page – above the fold, in living color – Gregory Townsend in all of his splendor leading one of the largest student rallies in the history of the county and probably the state. Gregory looked great. There was interest throughout the state. The battle of the blonds was going full steam. Jane Smith, the blonde superintendent, versus young blond Gregory Townsend, the high school senior. The county had never experienced anything quite like this before. A high school student challenging the superintendent was totally unheard of in this area of the state. History was being made in Dane County.

❖

Call it serendipity.

Call it synchronicity.

Call it providence.

Call it whatever you like, but this is what happened. A couple of months after Jane moved Monty Ray Hill from Riverplains High School to the district office, the local county chapter of the NAACP filed lawsuits against the Dane County Council and the Dane County School Board challenging the at-large method of election. In essence, what the NAACP was saying was that minorities could not get fair representation with at-large elections and the organization wanted to have single member districts for the county council and the county school board.

At the time of the lawsuits, anyone running for a seat on the school board or county council had to run county wide. Hence alliances were formed to help certain candidates win in precincts that they didn't reside in and wouldn't be able to carry otherwise. Single member districts would change all of that because the candidates would only have to campaign in the district in which they resided since only those voters in their districts would be eligible to vote for them.

The beauty of the NAACP school district lawsuit was that it would give us what we needed – a real chance at getting a completely new board. If the NAACP prevailed, and we had historical precedents that said it would, the legislative delegation would have to require completely new board elections for all nine seats. This would be only the second time in the history of the school board in Dane County that that had happened. The first time was when the board was instituted.

Now we were on the threshold of watching history being made in Dane County in a major way. Stacy, Louise, and I could hardly contain ourselves. Life was so good.

❖

My family has a history of being politically active educators so it was not surprising that my mother was very much involved in both lawsuits. She had been a member of the NAACP for as long as I could remember. Her commitment to the organization had increased noticeably when the state field director began coming to Lucien Heights for meetings to encourage the local membership to pursue single member districts as a way of increasing black representation in public office. The field director came for a couple of years before leaders of the Dane County chapter decided to sue the county council and the school board.

For our family, the lawsuits became reality the night one of the local NAACP officers, J. T. Mabry, called my mother and said that he needed to come by briefly concerning the potential case. My mother was in a good mood, although she was smiling a little nervously when he arrived. She said that J.T. was coming by with something for her to sign. He told her that he needed her signature and that it would just take a few minutes.

When J.T. arrived, he repeated that he really couldn't stay. He just needed her to sign two documents and he would have to go to collect other signatures. So, as my mother liked to say from that day on – and for many years as she told the story – "J.T. asked me to sign at the foot of the stairs, on the banister post, right in my hall. I signed because he told me my signature was needed." She always smiled when she described what happened when she signed the lawsuits. Of course the two documents were the two legal complaints, one against the county council and one against the school board. My mother made history that day standing at the end of our hall, signing the petitions on the banister post.

Several weeks later, the local paper, the *Herald*, ran a story about the lawsuits and featured the names of the signers of the lawsuits including my mother's name and the name of the president of the NAACP local chapter. Everyone seemed to notice my mother's name. Even though the article included many other names, Mildred Christianson's name was the one of the ones that stood out. It probably had to do with name recognition because she had been a teacher in Dane County Schools for 36 years before she retired. She spent the last nine years at Lucien Heights High School, so a lot of people knew her.

We received a phone call from Celeste about a week before the story was in the *Herald.* She chatted with me briefly and then asked to speak with my mother. I handed the phone to my mother and a few minutes later I heard laughter. After she hung up, my mother said that Celeste told her that when she was served with the lawsuit, she said. "Look at this. Mildred is suing me." Then they both laughed. The two of them had been friends for many years before the lawsuit and the friendship continued long after the lawsuit. They both understood only too well that the school board was one thing, but friendship was another.

❖

Adding to the political mix during this time was a movement by graduates of the former all black high school, Englewood High. The Englewood High grads wanted to change the name of the city's high school to Lucien Heights-Englewood High. Counties in other parts of the state had combined both of the pre-integration high school names to appease all segments of the population. In Dane County, not only had the names not been combined, but also the former black elementary schools were either completely demolished or the names were changed – for every single one. In effect, the black residents in Dane County lost all of the names of historical significance connected with their schools. The name change group wanted to preserve at least the name of the former black high school since they had lost the all the other names.

The impetus for the name change at this particular time was the recent passage of a school bond referendum, which allowed the district to build two new high schools, one in Riverplains and one in Lucien Heights. The building construction was progressing according to the timetable set forth originally which meant that the schools would be ready for occupancy by the beginning of Dr. Smith's second year as superintendent. The referendum had passed under her predecessor, but she was able to take credit tacitly since she would be the district's chief administrator when the schools opened. The public tended to have a short memory and would end up giving her credit regardless. Later she would be able to benefit from the former superintendent's hard work. But presently she was being asked to help change the name of the high school in Lucien Heights before the work was completed in order to open the new facility as Lucien Heights-Englewood High School.

One of the local white state politicians had talked with some of the grads while campaigning and promised to help them get the name changed. The grads were sincere and believed that he was too, but they soon learned that once he won reelection, his memory failed him and he had no recollection of having promised to assist them in their drive to change the name of the high school. The group realized that they would have to begin to mobilize their forces and request that the school board change the name of the high school. Accordingly, they wrote the school board and asked that they be given time to speak to the board to present their case for changing the name of the high school. Celeste graciously agreed to allow them to speak before the board. While she was gracious, some of the other board members were not and one older female board member, Jean Talbert, was especially outspoken against the grads and against any suggestion that the name would be changed. She was overheard saying something about "hell would freeze over first". Needless to say there was no love lost between this board member and the name change group.

Outside of the boardroom the groups were meeting and planning strategy. The name change group had a major rally that drew several hundred participants. It was held on the grassy area near the location of the building that was formerly Englewood High School. There was music and there were several articulate speakers. The speakers were all former graduates of Englewood High and included historians who explained how the land was originally obtained from a black owner to build the new Lucien Heights High School. The speaker maintained that the owner of the land sold it on the condition that the school would have both names to represent a unified community.

One speaker was such a great orator that he kept getting applause after virtually each sentence. The crowd loved him. He spoke of the need for the graduates to persevere and not be afraid of the consequences in economic terms. He told the assembly that some people were afraid if they publicly supported the movement to get the name of the high school changed that they would lose their jobs. His comment, "Remember, I was looking for a job when I got the one I have," rang a chord with the group. The group cheered loudly.

❖

The battle lines were clearly drawn.

On one side, there were grads requesting that the name of the high school be changed to include the name of the former black high school. On the other side, there was the school board.

On one side, there were high school students and county residents supporting the return of Monty Ray Hill back to Riverplains High as principal. On the other side, there was the school board.

On one side, there were members of the local chapter of the NAACP asking the school board to change its method of election from at-large to single member districts. On the other side, there was the school board.

Dane County had never, ever had so much controversy and conflict in all the years that anyone could remember.

Why blacks and whites got along well here in this county historically … at least that's what everyone always said.

The schools and the public always got along with the superintendent … at least that's what everyone always said – until now.

Now it seemed that everyone was out to get the school board for something or other. If it hadn't been so serious, it would have been laughable. The sleeping giant was waking up. Dane County was coming alive with explosive awareness.

CHAPTER 11

As all of the conflicts unfolded, I decided that since I was back at work, I could once again attend the school board meetings. I liked to be in the thick of things to see for myself what was actually going on. It seemed appropriate for my sons, Christian and Michael, to learn about local politics and school boards, so I invited them to come with me.

"Guys, I've decided that I need to begin keeping up with the school board again and so I'm going to start back going to the meetings the way I did before I got sick. Who would like to go with me?"

The older of the two, Christian, said, "Mom, I really don't have any interest in board meetings. After the way they treated you, I don't know why you would even want to go to those meetings." He was obviously declining.

"I'll go with you Mom. If Christian won't go with you, I will. I don't think you should be going to those meetings at night alone." My younger son, Michael, volunteered to accompany me so I wouldn't have to go alone. I was touched and pleased that I would have company.

As it turned out Michael loved the meetings! He was only in elementary school, but the entertainment value was just as high as the educational value for him and for me.

Michael understood that he had to have his homework done before the board meetings. But he willingly gave up TV, video games, and his computer twice each month to go with me to the meetings. In fact, he would sometimes ask me on a Tuesday afternoon whether or not there was a board meeting. He actually looked forward to the meetings. It was mother and son bonding and great quality time.

The school board of trustees met every 1st and 3rd Tuesday night of the month usually at 7 p.m. When Michael and I began going to the meetings, there were typically large groups of parents and other county residents standing outside beforehand and then crowding into the boardroom. Gradually the numbers increased to the point that there were so many people attending the meetings the board had to change the location of the meetings from the boardroom to a large area such a gym or a school cafeteria. The boardroom at the district office was suddenly much too small and the fire marshal refused to look the other way any longer.

Sometimes the parents would have presentations prepared or simply ask to be placed on the agenda to speak to the board. More often than not however, parents would rudely interrupt the meetings by shouting out or loudly calling a board member's name to take one of them to task or to just call attention to themselves. They loved to shout to Celeste:

"Madam Chairman, you can't do that!"

"Point of order, Madam Chairman!"

The parents' comments were invariably followed by the laughter and thunderous applause of their supporters in the audience.

It was wild.

"Mom, are they supposed to do that? Why are they shouting at Ms. Washington?" Michael often questioned the way the parents behaved toward Celeste in the meetings. He didn't understand their discourteous behavior.

At each meeting Michael observed the way Celeste chaired the board and he was tremendously impressed. He often said, "She's the only one on the board with any sense." He was definitely one of Celeste's loyal fans.

Things got wilder. The Englewood name change group began coming and presenting their case to the board on a regular basis. The group grew in numbers at each meeting. Their voices grew in volume at each meeting. They were becoming a lot like the Riverplains group.

I'll never forget one Tuesday night at the board meeting, the name change group held up a huge hand made sign that said, "Celeste Washington – Jane Smith Is Not Your Sister." I'm not sure what they meant by that, but the sign caught everyone's attention.

The whole thing was captured by the TV crew from one of the Columbia stations and shown all over the state on the 11 o'clock news that night. It was quite an experience.

❖

PUBS and the Riverplains groups were still working to dethrone Jane, as were the name change grads and others. By this time people all over Dane County just wanted something done about that 'Smith woman'. She was being perceived as a serious problem for the county's reputation … real bad PR. There was so much paranoia and back-biting in the schools that it's a wonder the teachers were able to teach anything. It's a credit to them that they were able to do their jobs in spite of so much confusion and controversy in the county. Morale was not only at an all time low in the schools, it had hit way past rock bottom.

Stacy had a major contact in the Statehouse who was keeping her posted on the progress of the school board legislation which would allow the board to be elected in single member districts rather than at-large. She could actually call that particular legislator and get an update on the legislation at any point in time. If he wasn't available, she would page him and he would call her back. That was great.

"Claire, I just told Louise, the three of us need to get together this afternoon to discuss the latest developments. We now know that Junior and Jane have a loyal supporter in the Statehouse trying to derail the whole process."

I asked, "You mean there is someone, a legislator, actually opposing the election changes?"

"Oh, yeah. But, he's slick. What he's saying is that he doesn't oppose single member districts; he just doesn't like the way the maps are drawn. Then he tries to delay making any changes so he can just tie it up … hoping the clock will keep on ticking and the session will be over."

"Can he do that and cause this to be delayed until next year?"

Stacy replied with confidence, "Not a chance. Our man says that the majority of the representatives support the map that J.T. Mabry and the NAACP want."

"I'm relieved to hear that. That's really good news. I thought we were going to have to deal with this current school board for another year. I'm not so sure if the county could survive that."

Then when the legislators drew the new maps for the school board districts, Louise, Stacy, and I went to the *Herald* office downtown to get copies, straight from the legislature. It was so exciting.

Louise came by my office and said to meet her at 4:00 that afternoon. "We're going to go in my car to pick up the new maps for the redistricting from the *Herald* office."

I was surprised. "They have copies? I thought the paper supported Junior and Jane."

"They do support the Smiths at the *Herald*, but the maps are coming straight from the Statehouse and they can't tamper with them or prevent from being made public."

Stacy then mentioned that there would be a town meeting to get public feedback on the proposed districts for the school board. "We don't need to attend that meeting, but I think that J.T. Mabry should definitely go and take good notes."

I assured her that I would let him know. "They won't be able to influence him. He has no use for Junior and Jane. He saw through them many years ago."

"You know Junior claims he has the black community in the palm of his hand."

"I heard, but the truth of the matter is that not all black people are fooled by him. Some of us know what is going on … that he just wants votes."

Stacy wanted to be sure that she understood what I was saying. "You mean there are some black people who don't support Jane?"

"Heck yeah. This thing with the Englewood name change has opened a lot of eyes. Jane refused to support the name change publicly after saying privately that she would."

"I know, but I thought that the Englewood group was blaming the board and not Jane."

"No, they know Jane is superintendent and she controls that board."

❖

Louise, Stacy, and I became a part of history in a way that few people realized. That afternoon the three of us got in Louise's car and headed for the *Herald* office. We were laughing and joking about how the district had unwittingly put the three of us together in a situation that worked to our advantage. We knew that we were privy to information that few others had, including some of the county politicians. We also knew that the ones who had the information didn't have the type of unusual network that we had or the countywide support base that we had. It was such an incredible time to be alive and to experience the feeling of actually making a difference ... actually being agents of major, positive change in the county. As we headed to the *Herald*, we were riding high. We were soaring.

We excitedly got the redistricting maps from the *Herald,* went to Kinko's and had copies made, and started our own distribution. I called J.T. Mabry, the NAACP officer, and told him about the new maps and he was anxious to get copies. He came by my house that evening and picked up the maps. He was thrilled to be getting them. The information gave him a heads up on what would be coming down the pike before the public had access to it. J.T. was able to look at the proposals and see which one would benefit the greatest number of people and which ones would be unacceptable. He was so appreciative. I let him know that Stacy had helped with it so that he would be aware that some of the so-called conservative whites in the county wanted to work with the entire community. There is definitely strength in numbers. J.T. was impressed and promised to do anything that he could to help the cause.

❖

J.T. had an opportunity to help sooner than he expected because the various groups were planning a massive protest for the next board meeting. This was going to be the protest to end all protests. They were expecting more than a thousand residents for the meeting. Stacy wanted the name change group to sit with PUBS and the Riverplains groups to show solidarity across racial and political lines for the entire county. I contacted J.T. and explained that we needed his assistance in getting as many people from the black community to come as possible. Then I called my cousin who was one of the main leaders of the name change group and asked if she could get in touch with the Englewood High grads to have a good showing for the meeting that Tuesday night.

It was unbelievable. Never in my wildest dreams could I have imagined what Michael and I would see that Tuesday night as we approached the middle school gym for the school board meeting.

There were city police all over the place.

There were 3 satellite trucks – one from the each of the Columbia TV stations.

There were dozens of high school students, black and white, marching with huge signs protesting Monty Ray's removal.

There were more people outside lined up to get in the meeting than I have ever seen in Dane County other than at a sporting event. Well over a thousand. That was the estimate on the news that night.

Michael and I were speechless. We both looked around at everything that was going on in amazement.

Was this Dane County?

When did things change?

How did we get to this point?

Security was unbelievably tight. Just as we got inside the gym and managed to find a place to sit, we realized that the board attorney was in the process of asking the sheriff's deputies to begin closing the doors to keep any more people from coming inside. He announced that the fire marshal was following the fire codes strictly and they could not exceed the maximum capacity for the gym. For those on the outside, it didn't seem to matter; they were still marching and chanting loudly in support of Monty Ray and against Jane Smith and the board.

The board attorney also stressed that no disruptions would be allowed, that anyone disrupting or interrupting the board would be ejected from the meeting and subject to arrest. He was serious.

The TV cameras were panning the room and their lights were so bright they were casting shadows all around the gym.

When the board attorney finally sat down, Celeste called the meeting to order. The air in the gym was full of the electricity of hopeful expectation. I wouldn't have missed this meeting for anything.

As soon as the board broke for a brief recess, the TV and newspaper reporters were like track stars rushing to interview members of the public, members of the board, protestors, anyone who would look good on the 11:00 news.

Then, something happened that I will never forget.

The PUBS group stood and began holding hands with the name change group and the two groups started singing *We Shall Overcome*. It was so beautiful. I had goose bumps and there were tears in my eyes. Who would ever have dreamed that something like this could happen in Dane County? A die-hard rural conservative white group holding hands with black Englewood High grads. It was better than a made-for-TV movie.

That was not serendipity.

That was not synchronicity.

That was providence.

❖

Louise liked to say that we had divided Dane County into thirds with each of us in charge of one major aspect of the master plan. Age wise, she was our fifty-something friend. Stacy was thirty-something and I was forty-something. We had nearly 100 years worth of experience between the three of us. Politically, Stacy had the PUBS contingent, I had the black contingent, and Louise had the 'whatever was left' contingent. The 'thirds' were not fixed or rigid and there was tremendous overlap because my network included lots of white contacts, associates and friends. Also Stacy's had some black individuals, primarily because her husband, Mark, had several black men in his employ and was well liked in the black community.

Our families had been feeling the effects of our jobs for some time and were so supportive or us, individually and as a threesome. I was divorced so my immediate family consisted of my mother and my two young sons. Louise didn't have children but she was married to a man who had strong political and family ties in the area. Stacy was married with three young daughters and her husband, Mark, was self-employed. There was one common thread among our adult family members; they were all well liked in their respective communities and in the greater community, the county.

Unlike some women we knew, we three did not have a problem spending as much time as we needed to on the phone. As a matter of fact, it was not uncommon for the three of us to be on the phone until well after midnight with one or the other. We talked almost every day, including weekends. Each day was full of new information and sometimes, new challenges which required an almost constant flow of communication between the three of us in order for us to stay abreast of all of the developments

But, the beauty of this was that the district had put us together in room 733 and now we were friends, close friends. We were able to take the unfortunate room assignment and turn it around so that the school district and the entire county could reap the benefits. We often laughed about it. Dr. Jane Smith kicked Louise and me out of the D.O. and put us in room 733 with another mover and shaker, Stacy.

Louise, Stacy, and I were in our own way a lot like the Bobo dolls that were popular many, many years ago. If you punched or pushed the Bobo doll it would bounce back. It had a weighted bottom and you could never knock it down. That was very much like the three of us. The district, meaning Jane and her minions, couldn't get us down. We just bounced back and each time we bounced back, it was with more determination and wisdom. We learned so much each day about people, about politics … about life.

The three of us were blessed with the confluence of events unparalleled in our lives. We had to take advantage of the community Zeitgeist. We had to go with the momentum and we had to work hard and with much due diligence. Clearly all of these wonderful opportunities would not last forever. We could never have predicted this. We could never have planned any of this to this level of perfection. People and events were coming together in such a profound and meaningful manner that we felt convinced that it was the great spirit of life smiling on us. It probably helped that we prayed everyday … sometimes together, but always individually and in our own way. It was an exciting time, a wonderfully productive time for each of us.

They put three politically astute, strong-willed women together in a highly undesirable situation at a time that the county was undergoing a metamorphosis of historic proportions. We put our individual expertise to work for the common good in a way that no one could have anticipated. It was simply amazing and so unbelievable. Two words come to mind: Divine Intervention.

CHAPTER 12

Then the final word came from the Statehouse. Dane County was going to have all new school board elections! Legislation was passed that changed the method of electing school board members in our county. This was unprecedented. The one thing that we needed to have happen was becoming a reality.

The new method of election required single member districts with lines drawn so that there was a high degree of probability that we would have at least two black trustees on the board. One of those potential black trustees would come from a district that included the Englewood precinct, my district.

Now, there was a solid chance that the county voters could do something about Dr. Jane Smith. People could actually elect board members who would listen to their constituents and not 'rubber stamp' everything that came from Jane's administration. The excitement was in the air throughout Dane County. All of our hard work was coming to fruition, but the real task lay ahead. We had to find candidates who could not only win, but who would go on the board and do what needed to be done: Fire Jane Smith.

❖

Dane County is divided by the Sandhills River into two main sections. The area of the county on the southern side of the river from Lucien Heights was considered as 'over the river' or 'across the river' in everyday conversations by local residents. The school district formally referred to it as the West Sandhills area.

I was friendly with one of the candidates, Susie Purle, who lived on the other side of the Sandhills River at the far end of the county past the Riverplains area, near Columbia County. She had served as a secretary for one of the elementary schools for several decades before retiring. I got to know her because I was assigned to her school as the psychologist. We would talk occasionally near the end of the day before I left and I knew that she was very displeased with the things that were being done by Jane Smith when she was the assistant superintendent. So when Jane became superintendent, Susie told me that after she retired she planned to run for the school board to fire Jane. I promised that I would support her and help her to carry the Englewood precinct. But now with single member districts, her campaign would be limited to her district, which was in the West Sandhills area. However, we remained friends and staunchly united in our goal of removing Jane from the top leadership position in the school district. This later turned out to be a very good thing.

Susie Purle was one of the first candidates to announce for the school board. She quickly established her position as an anti-Jane candidate and promised to do everything that she could to help her constituents to become involved in the schools again. The idea was to get rid of Jane and return the schools to the educators and communities. This theme was repeated by virtually all of the candidates for the new board to be elected.

A new district was created that included the area that Stacy and Mark lived in, which was a part of the larger area where Louise and her husband resided. Mark surprised everyone by deciding to run for the school board from the new district. We knew that he understood how dangerous Jane was and that we needed to have a different type of superintendent. In some ways, he was almost the perfect candidate.

Then as if lightning was striking, not twice, but three times, Stacy's best friend, Connie Scott, decided to run also. Connie lived on the Lucien Heights side of the river, but she lived far out in a rural area of the county about 15 miles from downtown in a community called Millbrick. If Connie, Mark, and Susie, were all elected we would have three votes to fire Jane. We needed two more for a majority on the nine-member board.

The West Sandhills area eventually generated a mega candidate, Gregory Townsend. It should not have surprised anyone, and it probably didn't, when Greg announced that he was running for the school board. He had turned 18 and was now legally old enough to run for public office in South Carolina. Greg was such a popular young man and so well known in the Riverplains area that no one thought that he would have any trouble being elected. Greg would bring the number of votes to oust Jane up to four. Now we needed one more member ... one more vote.

Celeste announced that she would seek reelection to the board. This was not unexpected. Most people felt good about Celeste continuing on the board because she brought a level of experience and competence that would be hard to find in a newly elected board member. We always believed that Celeste had the best interests of the children at heart. She liked to say that she represented all of the county, but especially poor whites and blacks.

One of Celeste's closest associates on the board was the woman who made the comment about 'hell freezing over' in opposition to the Englewood name change group. The woman, Jean Talbert, had been on the board as long as Celeste and was running for reelection in an attempt to hold on to her seat. Stacy's friend, Connie, was challenging Jean for the Millbrick seat. It was beginning to look like that seat would have one of the tightest races in the county.

The second 'black' seat on the board was being sought by two African-Americans: a man, Peter Jones, and a woman, Jessie Taylor. Of the two, Peter was a relative newcomer to politics. Peter was considered young compared to Jessie, who was a seasoned veteran of public life. He was actually close to the age of one of her children. She had retired from teaching, but was still active in the community. It was rumored that Peter had been hand picked by a group of county (white) Republicans. That was not unusual because most of the new candidates were supported by the county Republicans, even though the board seats were actually non-partisan. Anyway, this race was hotly contested. It was good for the county because unlike in the case of the Englewood precinct, the winner was not a foregone conclusion. The black community was now experiencing hard campaigning by and for black candidates, not just blacks campaigning hard for white candidates.

❖

Susie Purle called me at home one evening, as we got closer to the election. "Hey Claire, how're you doing? Remember when we were talking about my running for the board, you said that you would help out any way you could."

"Hi Susie. I remember. That was before we got single member districts and I wanted to help you downtown in my precinct."

"That's right, but I would like to get your help on this side of the river, in my district."

"I'll be glad to help if I can. What would you like for me to do?"

"I need you to call some of the people over here in the outer Riverplains area to ask them to vote for me."

"Sure, I can help with phone calls. Do you have a list of voters with their phone numbers?"

"Yeah, I have some special people that I think would be real impressed if you called them. Most of the parents know your name even if they don't know you personally. When you talk with them, they'll let their friends know. We could get a lot of support that way."

"If you can give me the names and phone numbers now, I can start calling tonight."

"Ok and don't forget to say "Dr." when you introduce yourself. I want them to recognize your name from the school district, you know, Dr. Claire Franklin."

I made the calls for Susie at her request, but I wanted to do something for Connie Scott as well. So, I called her and introduced myself as Stacy's friend.

"Hi Connie, this is Claire Franklin. I am psychologist with the school district and I work with a good friend of yours, Stacy Graves, at Vo-Teck."

"Oh. Hi Claire … Dr. Franklin. I'm so glad you called. I was planning on calling you. I have your name on my list of 'important people to call'."

We both laughed.

"I wanted to find out if you minded if I called some people that I know in your district to drum up support for you."

"If I mind! Girl, that's just what I need. I'd be honored if you would campaign for me. I don't know what to say. This is so nice of you."

I was relieved that she welcomed my help. "You've said all you need to say. I know that you support doing something about Jane, but is there anything else I need to know?"

"Just tell them that I will try to do everything I can to help the schools and to be a board member for all of the people. I don't have any special interests or hidden agendas. I'm just a plain country girl."

"You have children, don't you? Are they in school?"

"Yes, I have a son in second grade and my youngest son is going to kindergarten."

"Oh, you have two sons. So do I! We have that in common."

"We probably have more in common than we realize." Connie had a playful tone and we both laughed a second time. "I can't tell you how much I appreciate your helping me in this area."

"You are welcome. Consider it as part of my campaign contribution." Then I added with a chuckle, "I plan to make a financial one too."

After we hung up, I had a good feeling about Connie. We bonded almost instantly. I usually trusted my 'feelings' with people and I had a very good feeling about her.

❖

Louise, Stacy, and I worked the phones in the afternoons after work and in the evenings. It was important to contact all of the people that we knew throughout the county to solicit support for our candidates. One of the first questions that voters asked me was whether or not the people I endorsed were planning to get rid of Jane Smith. That seemed to be the most important question in the voters' minds. Would the person, if elected, be willing to vote to fire Jane. If the answer turned out to be a politically safe, middle of the road, response, chances were the person would lose the vote of the questioner. People wanted to hear it direct and clear: "Yes, my candidate will vote to fire Jane Smith" or "Yes, if elected, I promise to fire Jane Smith". We had never had a school board election quite like this before.

As the election heated up, several things became clear. With some of the hotly contested board seats, people were voting against certain candidates as much as they were voting for particular candidates in the election. A good example of this was the Millbrick seat. Most of the people that I talked with were determined to get Jean Talbert off the board. A lot of the members of the name change group lived in the Millbrick district and if they didn't live in the district, they had family and friends who did. So, the name of the game was to vote for Connie to be sure to vote against Jean. Some of the people that I called said that they didn't know Connie Scott, but surely she couldn't be as unwilling to listen to her constituents as Jean had been, so they were definitely voting against Jean. That meant that they were definitely voting for Connie, in their own way.

One woman that I called said it best, "Oh Dr. Franklin, I don't know Connie Scott, but I do know Jean Talbert and I have no use for her. If you ask me, she's as bad as Dr. Smith, maybe worse, because at least the board can stop Jane, but this woman has no one to make her do the right thing and she won't listen to the people in her community."

"Well we would appreciate it if you would vote for Connie."

"I'll vote for anyone you say if it means getting rid of Jean Talbert. That woman has no business being on the board."

"Oh, thank you so much."

"Don't mention it. We're going to show Jean Talbert what it feels like when 'hell freezes over'. Hah!"

❖

The race for Mark's district took an interesting turn when his only opponent sought the backing of Jane and Junior Smith. The man said he was taking the high road in campaigning by keeping an open mind – read: supporting Jane. We heard that he had been meeting with Jane and Junior planning his strategy. So because this was a critical seat, my mother volunteered to help Mark with the Lincoln Roads area of his district, which was predominately black.

A lot of the people in Lincoln Roads knew my mother and respected her opinion. One of our contacts was a close relative who had been politically active for many years in that area, Fanny Dee Burns. Fanny Dee loved my mother and talked with her by phone on a weekly basis. Now with the election in full gear, she called sometimes two or three times a week.

We almost forgot about the promise to help Mark Graves in Lincoln Roads until the week before the election. I suggested to my mother that we really didn't need to go out there, we could just check with Fanny Dee and have her campaign for Mark. She said no, we had given our word so we would honor that. I got flyers, signs, and posters from Stacy and put them in the car to take with us to Lincoln Roads. We went on a Saturday morning and encountered a lot of support from the people that we saw initially. Most people wanted the campaign flyers and some offered to put up a sign for Mark in their yard. So we were very upbeat when we got to Fanny Dee's house and certainly were not prepared for what we learned.

"Mr. Joe said everything's been changed", Fanny Dee told us with sadness in her voice.

I wondered who she was talking about so I asked, "Who is Mr. Joe?"

When Fanny Dee didn't say anything, I turned to my mother for an answer.

"Joe Bradshaw."

She explained further by telling me that he was the precinct chairman and he was responsible for distributing sample ballots and making important contacts within the Lincoln Roads community. The people in the precinct tended to vote as a block, so if "Mr. Joe" told them to vote for someone, they would do so without any hesitation.

My mother then asked Fanny Dee, "When did you find this out? Who do you think is behind this?"

Fanny Dee said she thought that Junior Smith had been out in Lincoln Roads meeting with some of the precinct officers and that he was going to 'make it worth their while' to get the vote for Mark's opponent. She went on to say that Mr. Joe had told the community that they shouldn't vote for Mark Graves, but they needed to vote for the other man. It sounded like down and dirty politics to me. Junior and Jane Smith had gotten the upper hand.

On the way home from Lincoln Roads, I expressed feelings of disappointment and distress. I had not ever come face to face with this side of politics before and I didn't know how to deal with it. I didn't want to call Stacy with the bad news. I knew that if Mark didn't carry Lincoln Roads, he would probably lose the election. My mother encouraged me to call her that evening and describe in detail what we had learned from Fanny Dee. So I did.

When I called Stacy, I began by saying that I was tired of politics and I didn't want to continue because the people were so fickle, we couldn't trust them. Stacy wanted to know why I was so discouraged. I said that I didn't know how to tell her, but the people in Lincoln Roads weren't going to vote for Mark. I then recounted the conversation with Fanny Dee. Instead of being angry, Stacy expressed gratitude to me for telling her. Her reaction was not what I had expected.

"You're not angry or hurt?"

"No", she said. "I'm glad that you went out there so now we know what's going on. It sounds to me like the money has hit the streets."

"Oh, I hadn't thought about that. I probably would never have thought about that here in Dane County. You think about that happening in major cities, but here in Podunk it is not something that I would have considered."

"Junior is known for that. Don't worry we still have time to do something about this. You went out there at the right time. Any later and it would have been too late by the time we found out. Don't feel bad, you've helped more than you know."

❖

Life was still smiling on us because a few days later Stacy called to thank me again and to bring me up to date on the Lincoln Roads situation. "Claire, everything has been taken care of."

"What do you mean?"

"For Mark's campaign. Guess who Mr. Joe works for?"

"I don't have a clue. Please don't ask me to guess."

"He works for Fred Eubanks. Fred is the owner of an oil company and Joe is one of his drivers."

"What? This sounds like fate is on our side."

"More than you can imagine. It gets better. Fred Eubanks loves Mark to death. He even tried to get Mark to run for the board long before he made up his mind."

"Are you serious?"

Stacy laughed and said, "Yes".

She continued with, "So Joe had to go back and tell the people in Lincoln Roads that it's back to Mark. They're going to vote for Mark now!"

"That's wonderful! I'll bet Junior and Jane never expected anything like this to happen. How did you make the connection?"

"I told Mark what you said about the report from Fanny Dee and he said he thought he recognize Joe's name. He was almost certain that he worked for Fred. When he went to Fred about it, he was told that we should not worry. From that we knew Fred would take care of it."

Life can be so good.

CHAPTER 13

Meanwhile, back in the schools …

The mood was not good. Fear was rampant. Virtually every school district employee was fearful for his or her job, with few exceptions. Even Jane's loyal supporters were subject to being reassigned, there was no job security or assignment security at any level, in any school, in any position.

This was evident by the fact that even Louise did not manage to escape Jane's long reach. Her job title was being changed to guidance counselor at Vo-Teck for the coming school year. She told me it was against her will. Jane put the word out that Louise had asked for it … to get away from me, of all things. Anyway, Louise was definitely not happy, but she suspected that it could have been worse, much worse.

I have never before felt the atmosphere in the school district so emotional and teachers as anxious as they were that spring just before the school year ended. My schools were on both ends of the county so I had a chance to travel all over the school district and get a feeling for the morale among the employees. Academy Street was one of my elementary schools that had had the same principal for over 20 years. Jane announced in late spring that she was reassigning him for the next year. The attitude of the faculty and staff seemed to reflect a general resignation to Jane's machinations.

One of the teachers came up to me and said, "I probably shouldn't say anything because you might be one of Dr. Smith's spies."

"Me, one of her spies? Are you kidding? Don't forget the first thing she did was to kick us out of the D.O."

"I know, I was just joking, but it's horrible what she did to our principal, Mr. Greene."

"What, is he being transferred?"

"Yes and he said Dr. Smith told him there was no need for him to question her because he's lucky to have a job."

"Lucky to have a job! Booker T. Greene is one of the best administrators in the school district. Jane knows that. No, she doesn't want him to challenge the move because it would add to conflict in the district. She probably wants people to think that he agreed with it. She knows she can't fire him."

"I don't know. He's devastated. Said she told him she was going to put a woman administrator here with the younger children because elementary children need a female principal. Have you ever heard of such?"

"No, and neither has Jane. When I first came to this county over ten years ago, all of the elementary principals were males. Female principals in Dane County are still unusual. No, Jane is trying to justify her spiteful actions. She never liked Mr. Greene anyway."

"He knows that. He told all of us she was out to get him."

That teacher who told me that was not one of her principal's supporters, but she recognized that what was happening to him was wrong.

When I went to the luncheon at the end of the year for the teachers and staff of Academy Street, the principal, Mr. Greene, was given a lot of sentimental gifts. Everyone at the luncheon heard heartfelt remarks by most of his teachers. He was so overcome with emotions that he cried. The man just cried. There was a wave of sadness that permeated the entire room. You know it is so sad when a grown man cries, a big strong, tough guy like that principal. There was not a dry eye in the room full of teachers.

As I left that elementary school that day after the luncheon, teachers and staff were still hugging and saying their goodbyes. It was such an emotionally wrenching experience. I wondered what kind of people are at the helm in this district. How can you do this to people and be impervious to their pain, their loss at being uprooted in this manner?

❖

I recall describing my experience at Academy Street Elementary School to a friend who was teaching at a rural county high school. She said, "I know exactly what you're talking about. We had the same kind of thing happen at our school. In fact, it was probably worse at our high school."

"What do you mean?"

"We lost both our principal and assistant principal … both of them, Mr. Jacks and Mr. Legrande."

"Both of them? I knew that your principal, Mr. Jacks, was being forced to retire by Dr. Smith, but what about your assistant principal? Is he being transferred?"

I liked Mr. Legrande and I was hoping that he was not another one of Jane Smith's casualties.

"No, it's worse than that. Our assistant principal is leaving the district. I believe he's going to the Low Country, maybe somewhere on the coast."

"Oh no! I had no idea! How awful! When did you find out?"

"We found out before the luncheon, but we heard the details at the luncheon itself. The reason we knew beforehand was because the Hospitality Committee took up money for two big gifts, one for our principal and one for the assistant. That's how we knew we were going to be losing both of our administrators."

"Everyone knew Jane hated your principal, Mr. Jacks, but what did she have against the assistant, Mr. Legrande?"

"We don't know, but Mr. Jacks got so emotional while he was speaking to the faculty and staff that he began crying. Then Mr. Legrande started crying too!"

"Both of them?"

"It was so sad. Everybody felt so bad for them both and for the school. Mr. Jacks could hardly talk he was so choked up and Mr. Legrande tried to take over and finish talking to the teachers and the next thing we knew he was crying too! And then he fell completely apart."

"How sad. What on earth is going to happen to Dane County?"

My friend couldn't answer that question. She did not have the answer.

We knew that Jane had forced Mr. Jacks to retire, but we later learned that Mr. Legrande, who was much younger than Mr. Jacks, was told if he didn't resign, his wife and other family members, who were district employees, would not be able to continue in Dane County. Can you imagine that? When Mr. Legrande was told to leave the school district, he relocated to a coastal city with his wife and children. No one fought Jane, except the psychologists.

Before all of this blew up, I had gone to Mr. Legrande to discuss what Jane was doing to the Special Services department. We had talked in the past about other issues and I felt that I could trust him. He listened patiently and then he said, "I'm going to give you my best advice."

"That's what I want you to do. That's why I came to you."

"Leave it alone. Don't try to do anything about Dr. Smith."

"Why not? You look like you're really serious."

"I am serious. She has worked many years putting this together and she is going to become superintendent. She has everything in place and all of her people positioned to give her the job. There's nothing you can do. Believe me. I know what I'm talking about."

I did believe Mr. Legrande and because of what he said, I thought he understood enough to steer clear of the conflict. I thought he was safe from Jane's spiteful actions. Shows you how much I knew.

❖

One of the custodians at Vo-Teck saw me in the hall and made it a point to tell me that he would miss working for us next year.

I questioned him gingerly. I thought he was just saying that because there was so much movement, people had started saying goodbye while they had the chance – just in case.

"Why? Where are you going?"

He replied, "I'm being transferred to the other end of the county and they're cutting my hours so the district can save on salaries."

"What?"

"I'm not the only one. The woman who cleans the building across the street is going to have to go to the Riverplains area and she doesn't have a car. She was riding with me out here to Vo-Teck, but I can't take her over the river 'cause I'm gonna be on the other end of the county. So she won't have a job – no transportation."

"Why are they moving you? What reason did they give you?"

"They said that they are overstaffed out here and they had to make some changes. I wasn't supposed to be moved and the director wanted to keep me, but one of the staff out here asked the head of maintenance to move me and let the other custodian stay here. I think he is friends with her husband."

"Do you know who did it? Who has connections in maintenance like that?"

"One of the teachers said she overheard the conversation with the lady from here and the guy over maintenance."

"Oh my goodness." I paused, I really didn't know what to say except to let him know that I felt for him and offer some advice. "I am sorry that you have to go all the way out in the country. Why don't you contact personnel and see if they will reconsider."

"I talked with Dr. Lyles, but she was nasty to me. She said I could take it or leave it."

After the custodian left, I wondered what kind of mean-spirited administrators could cause this kind of antagonism and grief throughout the district and not reconsider some of their administrative decisions or at the very least, take note and make adjustments. Not Jane and her minions. They just kept steamrolling right over people.

I felt like paraphrasing Tiny Tim from *A Christmas Carol*: God have mercy on us all … everyone.

❖

As if all of the grief and animosity heaped on the schools weren't enough, I learned from Peggy Shade, the new psychologist that the district finally hired, that Marlena told her that I was certified in German. That was confidential personnel information. Marlena had no business sharing that kind of information with another employee. But, the point was to send the message back to me that they were reviewing their options for me for the next school year, a veiled threat to put me in the classroom in a teaching position. Fortunately there was little or no interest in the school district to add German to the high school curriculum.

Being the helpful person that I try to be, I made the mistake of telling Peggy that she should have been offered a supplement when she was hired. Louise and I both had one. It wasn't much, several hundred dollars, but it was a part of the psychologists' salary schedule. When I was hired ten years earlier, it was included and Peggy should have had it as well. Louise took credit for the fact that we even got it. Apparently when she was formerly the special education director, before I came to Dane County; she insisted that the psychologists be given a supplement since they were district level personnel. Peggy was grateful for the information and eagerly scheduled another meeting with Marlena. The strange thing was that Marlena told her about the supplement when she was being interviewed for the job, but when she was hired, it was not on the contract. Now, she could go back to Marlena armed with the facts.

Not only did Peggy not get the supplement, but she ended up getting her wrist slapped by Jane through Marlena. Peggy said that Marlena told her that Dr. Smith had said to let her (Peggy) know that the board voted to discontinue that psychologists' supplement with all new psychologists hired. Then she wanted to know who had told her about the supplement. Peggy claimed that she reminded her that it was mentioned during her interview for the position with the district, but that somehow Marlena figured out that either Louise or I had discussed it with her. Soon thereafter, I received a call from Jane's secretary telling me that Jane wanted to see me as soon as possible. Her majesty was requesting my appearance. I had no choice. I had to go. My prayer partners and I began working overtime.

When I went for my meeting with Jane, we met on the first floor in the spacious room previously occupied by the former superintendent. It was obvious that Jane had added her own touches, but the room still felt like the other superintendent's office. You had the feeling of the need to respect the position if not the person. Jane smiled and offered me a seat, right beside her desk … so close that she could 'reach out and touch' me. I guess it was Behavior Management 101 – proximity control.

Jane began by telling me she was sorry that I had been hospitalized and then she reminded me of how she and Junior had come to Columbia to visit me. This was followed by a reminder that she had given me a copy of *Meditations for Women Who Work Too Much* and had written a personal message telling me to relax and enjoy life more, implying that I was a lot like her and we both needed to take time to smell the roses. I have to admit, not only was Jane a good politician, but she was usually politically correct.

"Oh, thank you so much again for the book. I'm still enjoying it. It is just what I need to remind me to be good to myself. You know, take care of Claire, not just the students and parents."

"You needed that. You're a single parent with two sons at home who depend on you. You need to let other people do their jobs. You can't take care of the world."

"Yes ma'am, you're right."

Sometimes Jane made a lot of sense.

Wait a minute, I thought, *was she threatening me with that comment about my sons depending on me?*

Jane wanted me to believe that she supported me. "I want you to know that I looked out for you when you were out on medical leave."

"You did?"

"Yes, I did. I don't mind telling you there were some who wanted to change you like we did Louise, but I said no to any suggestion that we move you to another position. I like you and I didn't want you to be hurt by your association with the wrong people. We need you in your position. You're a great role model for all of the children, but especially the black children."

"Yes ma'am."

"Well I'm going to give you some advice, the best advice I can give you right now. Stay away from Louise. She is nothing but trouble and she hasn't had a kind word to say about you. If you keep associating with her, you'll bring trouble on yourself and I know you don't want that."

"No ma'am."

"Oh, by the way. There's no need for you to try to help Dr. Shade or anyone else with personnel matters. That's what we have Dr. Lyles for – that's her job."

"Excuse me?"

"A word to the wise: Don't discuss salaries with Dr. Shade or anyone else. It's not your concern."

"Oh, all right."

"Now I know you have things to do and so do I, but I want you to know that my door is always open. I've enjoyed talking with you. You know you can come to see me anytime. Give my regards to your mother."

"Yes ma'am. Thank you."

I left. There was nothing further to say. Jane had said it all. She made it very clear what her position was and she left no doubt as to who was calling the shots. I couldn't wait to call Louise to tell her what Jane had said. I will admit though that I was a little leery of talking with her so soon after my meeting with Jane, not only because of the warning but also because of what she said about Louise bad mouthing me. The whole situation made me very uncomfortable.

However, I decided to go ahead and call Louise when I got home after I left Jane's office. "Hi. I wanted to talk with you after I had my visit with Jane today."

"That was today wasn't it? How did it go? What did she want with you?"

"Well, I didn't say very much. I listened politely and tried to limit my responses to 'yes or no ma'am'. Boy, she covered a lot of ground. The main thing she wanted to do was to tell me to stop being so 'helpful' and to steer clear of situations and people that she felt could create problems for me."

"Did she tell you to stay away from me?"

"I don't know how you guessed that, but as a matter of fact, she did, but Jane can't tell me who to associate with. She also said that I was not to discuss the issue of the salary supplement for psychologists with Peggy."

"I don't trust Peggy, so I agree with Jane. My advice is to have as little discussion with her as possible … about anything."

"Why don't you trust her?"

"She has that look of not wanting to be a psychologist. She wants to be an administrator and she looks down her nose at us because we're from South Carolina and she's from the great state of North Carolina."

"I'm not sure that she feels that way. I've talked with her about a lot of different things and she doesn't give me the impression that she has an elitist attitude."

"You always try to see the best in everyone, until it hits you in the face. But, I can tell you this; she's just biding her time since she just got here. You watch. She's going to try to become director."

"Why do you think Jane told me to stay away from you? She knows that we are friends."

"It's the oldest trick in the book. It's called divide and conquer."

"I realize that, but she should know that it won't work."

"She doesn't want the two of us to work together because we might be able to get something done about her. That's all that is."

"She claims that you asked to be transferred out of Psychological Services so you could get away from me."

After I told Louise what Jane had said, she became indignant and asked, "Does that make any sense? Why would I demote myself?"

"I don't think she meant that you demoted yourself; I think it goes back to what Dr. Anderson offered you – a type of administrative assistant to the Vo-Teck director. But, if you will recall, I told you that was not going to happen. It was just a ploy to make you think that you could eventually become an administrator."

Louise's tone changed visibly. She had that slow, deliberate manner of speaking that emphasized each word. That was a signal to me that she was not pleased about my comments. "You've said that all along."

"I know, but you didn't seem too interested in my opinion. I felt that it has put strain on the friendship."

"Well, there's nothing I can do about it now. I can't undo it and I still believe that Jane demoted me for spite."

That conversation effectively ended any and all discussion about the reason for Louise's (involuntary) transfer from Psychological Services for the district to counselor for Vo-Teck. We never spoke about it again

CHAPTER 14

The night of the election, Michael and I went to the county courthouse to hear the results firsthand instead of finding out from TV. We ended up sitting with Susie Purle and her family. There was an air of anxiousness in the room that night. So many people were there who had never been involved in politics before and now they were sitting in the main courtroom of the county courthouse waiting for Junior Smith to read the elections numbers. Junior always read the results because he was the county election chairman and had been in that position for many, many years.

There we were sitting in the courthouse waiting for the results to start coming in. Susie Purle was to my right with her family. She introduced me to her daughter and then leaned over and asked, "Do you know Howard Moore?"

"No, I don't believe we've ever met".

Susie turned to the row behind her and said, "Howard, this is Dr. Claire Franklin. She worked real hard for me. In fact, Claire helped several of us."

Howard shook my hand. He was a rugged outdoors type of man who looked ill at ease in the courthouse. He looked as if he would have been much more at home anywhere on the outside, maybe camping or hunting. Then it hit me and I commented, "I believe I remember you from Ebenezer Baptist the night they had the forum for the board candidates."

He laughed, a deep hearty laugh and said, "That was the night I thought I was going choke to death with that tie on. I felt like I couldn't breathe. It kept getting tighter and tighter and I kept jerking on it trying to loosen it up. I was so glad to get it off when that meeting was over!"

I laughed too. "I could tell you weren't very comfortable."

Susie laughed and slapped his leg with one of her flyers saying, "Oh Howard, I declare …."

Howard continued to smile, taking the good-natured teasing in stride.

We were interrupted by Junior making a big production of checking his microphone by tapping on it and blowing into it loudly. He got our attention. I looked over at Susie. I could tell she was nervous.

Then I looked around the room to see if I recognized any of the other candidates. I did see some of the incumbents, but there were so many people it was difficult to distinguish the faces well.

The results for Susie's race were the first to be announced. She won easily. Her opponent didn't even have a third of the vote. Susie jumped up screaming when her victory was assured. The room seemed to jump up with her and the whole place exploded with cheers. Everyone around me was hugging each other and smiling. Howard won also, though not as easily. But a win is a win.

I began to get a tremendous surge of elation. I had a very strong feeling that the night was going to be full of spectacular wins. It was. Peter Jones won the second 'black' seat on the board which meant that he and Celeste were also making history in Dane County. This was the first time that the school board of trustees would have two black members.

All of the candidates that Stacy, Louise, and I supported won their individual races. That meant that eight out of the nine board members were elected that night for the first time. The courthouse was full of jubilation. It seemed that all of the people there in the courtroom were celebrating victories.

Junior's voice grew weary by the end of the night, as it was sinking in that the board which had named Jane superintendent was no more. It was gone. Jean Talbert lost her seat and Fred Hines was not re-elected. The only one who survived from the old board was Celeste. That didn't surprise anyone, nor did it bother anyone. If we had to have someone from the old board get re-elected, Celeste was the ideal person. I thought of this new board as "the people's board".

The election that night was covered statewide. History was being made. Media coverage was extensive and there were TV cameras and reporters all around the room. Dane County had the distinction of having two of the youngest board members ever elected in the entire state. Greg Townsend was one of them.

As Michael and I headed home, I wondered what was next. We had several months until the first of January of the coming year when the newly elected board members would be installed. A lot could happen before then.

And, as it turned out, a lot did happen. Jane's lame duck board went crazy. They started doing things to make it hard for the incoming board. One thing that they did that upset the entire community was to give Jane an extended contract. They conducted a last minute evaluation and she earned a superior rating overall. The board then used that to justify the contract extension. That board knew that the most of the newly elected members had run on a campaign promise of firing Jane, so they extended her contract to make it difficult for the new board to get rid of her.

Nevertheless, there was a mood of optimism about the future of the school district after the elections. People understood that even with the lame duck board still at the helm for a few months, there were major changes coming with the New Year. Things were definitely going to get better. The word was out on the person who would probably become the board chairman. The name that everyone heard was Dewey Fowler, a local businessman who represented the downtown area of Lucien Heights. Stacy's husband, Mark, was being mentioned as the vice-chairman. Things were definitely going to be different.

❖

Several weeks after the school board elections in November, Connie and Stacy decided that as the team that had worked so hard to defeat the old board and elect 'the people's board', we needed to get together to officially celebrate our successful outcome. Stacy called me with the details:

"Hi Claire, I know you're like us … still feeling good about the elections. Mark and I are so excited. We have said it many times, but I don't believe we can thank you enough for your help. Near the end, you made a big difference."

"Stacy, I've told you before, you don't have to keep thanking me, we worked together as a team."

"I know. But, thank you anyway. The reason that I called is because I wanted to let you know that Connie Scott and I were talking about all of us getting together for some kind of celebration. We thought we could all go to dinner in Columbia."

"Sounds good. Who are 'all of us'?"

"You, Louise, Connie, Tricia, and me. Just a night out with the girls in celebration of our victories and in recognition of all of our hard work."

"I'd love to be a part of that. Just tell me where and when."

"What do you think about the Red Lobster in Columbia off of Two Notch … maybe next Friday?"

"Great! I love seafood. That's a good choice. I've eaten there with my family more times than I can count."

"I'm going to drive, so you can ride with me. Connie and Louise are going to leave their cars at my house and I'll pick up Tricia and then you. We'll take my van."

"This sounds like fun!"

We actually had a great time. On the ride over to Columbia, I had a chance to talk with Connie and Tricia and I was able to learn so much more about them. They both had a good sense of humor although Connie had more of a dry wit. The five of us laughed and talked about Jane and our experiences since she became superintendent. We all laughed … and laughed … and then laughed some more. What a fun night. We all got together so well, it was hard to believe that we had only been friends for just a few months.

Of all the people that we were involved with in the drive to get rid of Jane, I'd have to rank Tricia Langley as the one who provided the most levity. Connie and Tricia had been friends for some time because of the parents' groups at Canaan Elementary, where their children attended school. The two of them put their heads together on so many issues that it was only natural that they would join forces against Jane Smith. What started out as a simple act of seeking information turned into a saga that almost brought the district to its knees.

In the middle of the shared principal controversy, Stacy had asked Tricia to go to the D.O. and ask for some specific financial information from Jane. Tricia approached the administration as a Canaan parent asking questions because she was trying to learn about school district operations. As it turned out, Tricia was a natural actress who could improvise in a matter of seconds. We heard that she ended up creating such a big commotion in the building the first time she went that she and Stacy decided that she had to go back again … and again … and again to harass them for more and more information. Each time she entered the building, the front desk would alert Jane's office so they could try to find reasons to deny her access to records and discourage her from asking questions. The office staff had strict orders to warn Jane whenever 'that Langley woman' was in the building. When Tricia talked about her visits to the D.O. with us afterwards, it was always hilarious. She was so funny. Needless to say, Jane despised her. Tricia stopped the visits after the election, but they provided some desperately needed comic relief during some of the more challenging times.

CHAPTER 15

Something was bound to happen. The newly elected board members were feeling so upbeat. So it should not have been a surprise when Stacy called one evening and said, “I have some horrible news!”

“What on earth has happened now? Is this Jane related?”

Her voice sounded as if she was on the verge of tears, “Yes, it’s all Jane.”

“What’d she do now?”

“She’s closing Canaan Elementary.”

“Why? How can she justify closing an entire school just like that?”

“She said that the student population has decreased to the point that it is not profitable for the district to keep it open.”

“What about Cedar Hills Elementary? It’s on the far end of the county and the population has always been pathetically low. What's she going to do about that school?"

"Well you know Junior is from Cedar Hills so he won't allow anything to happen to the school no matter how few students they have."

"Oh, I had forgotten about that. She'll never touch Junior's hometown."

"But Canaan is still not the smallest even if you don't include Cedar Hills."

It still did not make sense to me. "I know, so why did Jane suddenly decide that Canaan needed to be closed?"

"Spite. She's mad because Mark got elected so she wants to show him that she can close our school in our community."

Mark was such a rising star.

"That really is mean. Do you think the board will allow her to get away with this?"

"Yes. They'll do whatever she tells them to. There's not a lick of sense among that whole crowd. And besides, they're mad too since all of the incumbents who ran were defeated."

"Celeste wasn't."

"Yeah, you're right. But Celeste will support Jane, no matter what."

"She sure will. What can be done about this? Is it a done deal?"

"Uh-huh. It's just a matter of the board voting to approve it."

"They're going to close a perfectly good school just because Jane is spiteful. That makes no sense whatsoever."

Just when we thought things might be getting better.

Stacy interrupted my brief reverie with a bit of local history. "You need to remember that Junior used to be principal at Canaan Elementary."

"I had forgotten about that. How long was he there?"

"Long enough to get mad with the community and get out."

"So he asked to be reassigned to Broadwater Elementary?"

"No, he was principal at both schools at the same time."

"He was? So this share-a-principal concept is not new?" I hadn't known that the district had done something like that once before. But then it made sense. Every thing in education goes in cycles.

Stacy continued, "No, Junior used to travel between the schools. He always liked Broadwater better, even when he first started."

"He told me a long time ago that Canaan was in a racist area."

"Now how would he know? He's such a bigot himself."

"Junior? I never got that impression." I couldn't understand how Stacy could say that about him.

Her explanation was simple. "He wants you to think that he gets along well with the black community."

"When he was principal at Broadwater, we used to talk a lot. He told me the people were terrible out in Canaan."

"That's because he never liked the Canaan community. The people saw him for who and what he was."

"What? He told me that one year he had to walk on one side of the Ms. Henning, who was black, and a white teacher walked on the other side to get her out of the school safely. He said that some of the whites in the Canaan community were threatening her because she was black and they didn't want her in that school."

"He probably tried to make you believe the Klan was behind it."

"Yes. I think he did. He said that was after they first integrated."

"He lied. That never happened."

Stacy sounded disgusted about the fabrication. I was hoping that she wasn't put out with me for appearing gullible by believing Junior. But I wondered if she had the facts straight. Junior had been very convincing. "How do you know?" I asked as I continued my defense of him.

"Junior has told that same lie to other people – the same lie."

"Are you serious?"

"Yes I'm serious. I was at the school the first day he started there as principal. I know what happened. He lied to you to impress you."

"To impress me?" Now Stacy had me confused. I couldn't think of any reason why Junior would want to impress me.

"Yeah, that's the way Junior is. He wants certain blacks to think he's so open-minded."

"I knew Jane was phony, but I thought Junior was sincere."

"He's not any better than she is."

Still defending him, I said, "Junior told me that he grew up with blacks around who were like brothers to him."

"They probably worked for his daddy. Don't you let Junior fool you."

"So he wants Canaan Elementary closed too?" I hated to ask, but I wanted to know what Stacy thought.

"Too? He's probably the reason Jane decided to do it. I'm sure he's also mad about Lincoln Roads. You know Mark carried that precinct."

"My goodness. Is there no limit to what these people will do?"

"Louise knows them real well too and she said that they'll hold a grudge for years and years. Then just when they think you have forgotten about it, they'll try to pay you back."

"I had no idea that Junior was like that too. I am so disappointed. They would close a school, uproot children and bus them somewhere else just to get back at the Canaan community."

Stacy quickly gave me a sharp reminder. "And Mark. Don't forget Mark."

"Oh I know, to get back at Mark too. Where are the children going to go to school next year ... to Broadwater Elementary with Junior?"

"No, they're going to bus them into town to Lucien Heights Elementary."

"All the way into town? How many miles is that?"

Stacy was quite matter-of-fact in her reply. "About 20-25 miles round trip depending on where they live."

It was hard to fathom that anyone, including Junior and Jane, would do something like that to children simply because they could. "That's a lot of riding for those young children just so Jane and Junior can spite Mark."

"You think they care? They'd send them to west hell if they had to – just to have their way and get back at the community."

"Something's got to be done; maybe we can get the people in Canaan to protest."

"Don't you worry. We're already working on that. You think that Riverplains crowd has been getting a lot of attention … just wait until the board has to deal with the Canaan parents."

"Oh my goodness! This whole situation is so crazy."

"People are gonna do what they have to do. They're not gonna roll over and let Jane get away with taking away an important piece of the community without a fight."

"The school's important to the community?"

"It's the hub of the Canaan community. Everything is centered there. It's like a town hall, a school, everything all in one."

"I didn't know that." There was obviously a lot that I didn't know about some of the rural communities in Dane County. But, thanks to Stacy I was on my way to becoming better informed about the various areas of the county.

Stacy explained, "Junior and Jane know it. That's why they're closing the school. It would hurt that entire part of the county."

"What about Cedar Hills? Is it the same up there?"

"No, they have a town government. It's tiny but they have it nonetheless. We don't have anything but the school."

"That's cruel. How can they continue to do things like that?"

"Because they're mean. It comes naturally to those two."

❖

On the heels of that came the next salvo. Jane attacked the teachers at the three Lucien Heights elementary schools. Every single teacher in the three city schools was told that they would be transferred for the coming year. Jane was planning a fruit basket turnover of the faculties at the three elementary schools in Lucien Heights. I didn't know about it until one of my friends at Academy Street Elementary stopped me in the hall of the school one day and asked, "Where do you think I'll end up next year?"

"I don't know. I don't think Jane is targeting teachers right now; she's too busy disrupting entire communities and closing their schools."

The woman replied, "It's obvious you haven't heard what she's requiring us to do."

"No, I haven't. Seriously, are the teachers being targeted now?"

"Yes, they are … big time."

"How so?"

"Dr. Smith has said that she wants to move teachers around in the three city elementary schools to balance out strong and weak teachers."

"Just how does she propose to do that?"

"She has sent out school preference questionnaires to all the teachers. We have to list the three schools in order of preference and grade level that we want."

"When did all of this happen and why so close to the end of school?"

"I don't know why they waited so late in the year, but I do know that she said we would know before we leave for summer vacation."

"Oh, so they will make the assignments before school closes."

"Yeah, and she said that we may not get our first choice, but not to worry they were going to try to accommodate all preferences."

"Jane is saying all of this?"

"No, she doing it and Lyles is saying it. They've got to keep up appearances, you know, since Lyles is the personnel director."

"My goodness! There is truly no end to this madness."

❖

Jane had managed to do something to every area of the county. No area was immune or even safe from her. Why would she want to upset the teachers all over Lucien Heights and Dane County? It made no sense. It just made people angry with her and frustrated over the fact that they were powerless to do anything.

While I pondered the fate of the district, I recalled that first board meeting when Jane became superintendent and Canaan Elementary was on the agenda for the share-a-principal plan. I was outside the administration building talking with some of the other individuals as we were all taking a break while the board was in executive session – presumably moving Mr. Lennix among other things. One of the people that I talked with was Margaret Beech, the principal at Canaan. I asked her:

"Do you know what changes they're planning tonight?"

She said, "No, that's why I'm here … to avoid unpleasant surprises."

"What have you heard?"

"Just that Jane was going to move some administrators around, but it doesn't look now as if that's going to happen."

"No, it doesn't. But we heard a rumor that they were going to move the psychologists out of the administration building."

"Where would you go?"

"I don't know. None of the schools have any room."

"Well, if you need a place to call your home base, you can use a portion of one of the portables out back. We'll clean it up for you and give you your own area."

"Thank you, that is so generous of you. But I'm hoping I won't need to take you up on it."

"If you do, don't hesitate to let me know."

Margaret left soon thereafter because it was after midnight and the board wasn't showing any signs of coming back to the boardroom any time soon. I didn't think too much about our conversation until I was talking with Louise the next evening and she asked me if I had heard about what happened to poor Margaret Beech.

"No, what happened? I talked with her last night and everything seemed to be all right."

"You know how late it was when the board finally came back after that extended executive session."

"I remember quite well. I'm still tired from being up till the middle of the night."

"Well apparently after we left, Jane announced the principals for the share-a-principal schools. Margaret Beech was not named. Some new 'Dr. Somebody or Other' from out of town got Canaan and Broadwater."

"Noooo!"

"Yes, I just talked with one of Margaret's good friends. She said that Margaret left the board meeting and went home and went to bed. Then Margaret got a call from someone at the D.O. in the middle of the night congratulating her on her new position."

"What new position?"

"She's now the new assistant principal at Lucien Heights Elementary."

"What? That's a demotion!"

"I know. Can you imagine someone waking you up from a sound sleep to tell you that you've been demoted?"

"Margaret didn't have any idea it was going to happen? I thought she and Jane ran in the same political circles."

"They do, but Jane didn't tell her about the demotion. It hit Margaret like a bolt out of the blue."

"She was saying that I could come to Canaan if necessary. She would find space for me."

"She not finding space for anybody at Canaan anymore, she's not going to be there herself."

"Why do you suppose Jane did that to her? I thought they were friends."

"I heard the Canaan parents were mad with her because they said she was a weak disciplinarian. She was a great teacher, but not such a good administrator. Said she wanted to teach the children when they were sent to the office instead of disciplining them."

"Didn't they know that before they promoted her?"

"She had the backing of the PTO and the School Improvement Council. Our friends Stacy and Tricia were calling the shots. They wanted someone new."

"Be careful what you ask for. Now they have a new principal, but they have to share this new lady."

"Yup."

We should have been able to see the handwriting on the wall with the way that Jane treated Margaret Beech that night. The entire change was handled poorly, but no one seemed to be willing to do anything about it at the time. Now Jane was continuing what she started less than a year ago and was obviously determined to force her will on the district's employees and on the community at large.

❖

The horror stories with administrators continued.

I parked my car in the area in front of the building at Academy Street Elementary and got out and headed across the parking lot to go into the school when I saw the principal, Mr. Greene, coming out. He spoke hurriedly as if preoccupied and didn't smile which was unusual. But, I went on in the building and walked into the office. As soon as I entered, the secretary looked at me with fear in her eyes and said, "Hi Dr. Franklin. Did you see Mr. Greene as you were coming in?"

"Yes, I did. He was headed out to the parking lot."

"He's going to the district office. He's very upset."

"I thought that there was something wrong. He didn't seem to be himself."

"He doesn't need to go up there as upset as he is. Dr. Smith called and upset him."

"She did? Do you want me to try to catch him?"

"Would you please?"

"Yes." I took off immediately and ran outside to try to catch him.

"Mr. Greene! Mr. Greene!" I called out to him as he was getting in his truck.

He stopped and looked in my direction. "Yes?"

"Do you have a minute?"

"I've got to go to the district office to see Dr. Smith. Can we talk when I get back?"

I had to stop him at all costs. "I'm afraid not sir. This is urgent!"

"Oh ... alright, but I don't have a lot of time."

"Thank you so much. You don't know how much I appreciate this."

He came back and met me at the door. We walked in together and headed for his office. The secretary mouthed the words, "Thank you" as I passed her desk.

Once we got inside his office, I told him that I was worried about him, that he seemed upset about something.

"I'm so angry. Dr. Smith called here saying she wants me to come at once to talk with her about a complaint that she just got from a parent. It's just harassment. She's trying to make me say or do something so that they will have grounds to terminate me."

"I knew something was wrong. Don't you think you need to calm down before you go up there?"

"No, I'm going to let her have it! I'm going to tell her what I think about the so-called complaint and the way she has been harassing me ever since she became superintendent."

"That's fine, but I think that you need to consider your situation and not let her provoke you into doing something that you will regret."

"I guess you're right. What do you think I should do?"

"Do you have a Bible?"

"Yes, I keep one down here." He opened his personal desk file drawer and took the Bible out.

"Turn to Psalm 37," I instructed.

He turned to the scripture and then looked up at me.

I sensed what he was thinking and said, "I know it's long, but it's perfect for times like this. I read it every night just to be able to deal with Jane Smith. 'Do not fret over evildoers....'"

"Yes, that's the first line. Do you want me to read all of it?"

"Yes, the entire Psalm. You will be amazed at the difference in the way you feel after you read it."

He read it in its entirety, sitting there at his desk.

Then when Mr. Greene finished reading Psalm 37, I made another request, "Please try not to let her get you to do anything rash while you are in her office."

"Thanks for the advice and scripture. I'm going to pray on the way over too. I do feel much better."

"Good. I'll wait here at the school until you get back. I have to meet with a teacher, but I'll come back to the office area when I finish in the classroom and just wait for you to return."

After Mr. Greene left I went back out to the main office and told his secretary what had happened. She looked so relieved. "I thought he was calmer when he left just now. Thank you so much Dr. Franklin."

Later that morning when Mr. Greene returned, I had chance to find out what happened at the D.O. with Dr. Smith. I asked him, "Were you able to stay calm and not say the wrong thing?"

"I was. Dr. Smith had one of the men from downstairs meeting with us, I guess as a witness. I got so mad at one point I started to take him out!"

"But you didn't?"

"No, I did not. I almost had to sit on my hands to keep from punching him, but I didn't do anything to him or anyone else."

"Great!" I said with a gigantic smile.

"I want to thank you for helping me to stay professional and in control of my emotions this morning."

"You're welcome. I had to return the favor. You know how many times I have come here for shelter and support, when I no longer had my own office."

He smiled and said, "One good deed deserves another."

❖

In another situation, we heard that one of the secondary principals went to Dr. Jane Smith and begged her not to change him from the city schools because he and his wife had just had a new baby and he needed to be in the Lucien Heights area to be close to his family. He allegedly lost all pride and got on his knees to beg the woman to allow him to stay in town. She promised him that she would not change him; said she understood and had compassion for his circumstances. He got up off his knees and wiped his eyes and thanked her profusely. We were told he left her office a happy man. He was relieved and full of hope; he would be able to stay at his school in town.

I believe Jane was a master at instilling trust and thereby creating a false sense of security. She lied to that principal. He found out a few days later when the letter came from Marlena Lyles in personnel telling him of his new assignment for the coming year. You can imagine where he was transferred. That's right. His new school was on the far end of the northern part of the county, way out past Millbrick and almost to Cedar Hills … as far as Jane could send him. She was all heart, one of a kind.

CHAPTER 16

Near the completion of Jane Smith's first year as superintendent, the administration announced that the share-a-principal plan would be discontinued at the end of the school year. Once the administration decided to close Canaan Elementary, they probably knew that they had to do something about the shared principal plan. With Canaan closing, it meant the principal who was formerly shared would then have just one school. The district would only have one remaining shared principal, who would be left at two schools. That simply would not work. Even Jane understood that.

The Monty Ray Hill controversy apparently died of natural causes. Dr. Smith never allowed Monty Ray to return to Riverplains High School even though when she originally moved him to the D.O. it caused such an uproar in the county and created negative publicity statewide that the effects were still being felt. She was determined to have her way and the board was guilty of enabling her. By the end of that first school year with Jane Smith as superintendent, Monty Ray Hill, an unlikely local celebrity, quietly retired only to come back in the fall as an assistant principal at Riverplains Middle School.

Monty Ray Hill's involuntary transfer was the catalyst for a groundswell of support for him that led to a major change in the way the Dane County public dealt with controversy. The county saw so much media attention and there were so many rallies and meetings that the area could no longer be described as apathetic. To top it off, at least one new board member came directly out of the Monty Ray Hill affair and ended up becoming the youngest person ever elected to a school board in the state.

The lame duck school board decided to throw a bone to the name change group by offering to build a memorial to Englewood High School on the actual site of the former school. The members of the name change group did not have a chance to respond as a body to the board's plan. It was presented at one of the last meetings of that board and followed-up by an article in the *Herald* the next day. According to the board chairman, Celeste Washington, the memorial was a compromise that would allow the name change group to honor the historical tradition of Englewood even if it did not allow for the hyphenated name change of the high school that the group was seeking.

By the time the decision was made to place a memorial on the Englewood site, a large number of the individuals who had been a part of the name change group were no longer actively involved. There were rumors that some of the participants had literally had their job security threatened. Allegedly employees of the two major industries in Dane County were told to stop pushing for the name change or they could look for employment elsewhere.

Clearly there was a factual basis for the message given to the crowd at the rally earlier in the year when the speaker admonished the group not to be intimidated by employers or fear for their jobs.

For all practical purposes, the major conflicts of the school board vs. the community were resolved by the end of Dr. Jane Smith's first year. The resolutions were not necessarily satisfactory to all concerned, but they were put in place nonetheless by a board that would soon cease to exist and were not challenged by the community. Perhaps things appeared to have become more harmonious only because the various groups were waiting for their newly elected board members to take office and make a change in the office of the superintendent.

CHAPTER 17

And so life continues …

After Louise was transferred to Vo-Teck for the coming school year, she was able to keep the same office area in her new position as guidance counselor. What I didn't know until the end of that first year at Vo-Teck was that Jane had plans to move me out of my office again and send me to yet another area. I found out by accident from one of the custodians who was in the process of cleaning the classroom that adjoined my office. He knocked on my door and asked when was my last day.

"Oh, we normally stay two weeks after the teachers leave. Why do you want to know?"

"I have to do the floors in this area and I wanted to do yours while I was down here. But, if you're going to be here after school closes it won't be a problem."

Then he asked me what I thought was a strange question. "When are you going to move your things out?"

"Excuse me?" I didn't have the foggiest of what he was talking about.

He continued, "They told me in the office that you're going to have to move out of here and go someplace else."

I explained, "That can't be right. Dr. Smith approved this office for my use at the beginning of the year."

"Yes ma'am, I know, but they said you won't be able to stay here in this office for next year."

"Why not?

"The nurses want their office back."

"They do? So the district's going to move me out? Do you happen to know where they're going to move me?"

"I don't know, I think up there near the Adult Education office."

I wondered if he actually knew something that I didn't. But I simply said, "There aren't any offices up there other than in Adult Ed."

"They're going to change one of those large classrooms into an office area."

"Oh. I don't understand why no one mentioned this to me."

His manner and expression shifted to the patience of realization. For the first time he seemed to grasp that I truly did not know anything about the proposed move. He looked at me sympathetically and said, "Your friend, Ms. Ryan, knew about it."

"She did? How do you know that?"

"That's what they told me in the office. They said she and the woman who's over nursing are real good friends and they planned it."

"Hmm … I know there is a family connection, but I'm not sure they're good friends … but what do I know?

They probably are good friends and they probably did plan it. I just wish they had let me in on the plans."

"Yes ma'am. Don't worry about the floor. I can do that anytime after you move up front." He sounded as if he felt sorry for me.

"I appreciate your telling me what you heard."

"Oh you're welcome. Some of us were saying it's not right that you have to move and the other lady gets to keep her office."

"That's ok. She's going to working with Vo-Teck next year anyway, so she probably is going to stay in her office because of that."

After the custodian left, I thought about the prospect of having to move again without any real information, except that I would be going up front. And Louise ... Naturally I never said anything to her about what I had been told by the custodian. We still had work to do with the board and I had to give that priority.

I called Celeste Washington that evening to ask if she knew anything about my having to move again. Celeste was well aware of what was going on with the office space. She said, "They're going to put the psychologists back with Special Services."

"They are? When was this decided?"

"We had so many complaints and problems with the psychologists being one place and Special Services being another that Jane decided to put everybody together at Vo-Teck."

"Special Services is coming out to Vo-Teck? The department is leaving the administration building?"

"Yes, I told Jane that it wasn't right for the psychologists to have to go back forth from Vo-Teck to the district office when you have to run all over the county trying to do your jobs in the schools. I told her that the whole department needed to be at Vo-Teck."

"How does the new director of Special Services feel about the move?"

"I don't give a flying flip how she feels. The department needs to be in one central, unified location. You all can't work like that ... It's not efficient."

I laughed. "I'll bet the secretary and director don't want to have to come out to Vo-Teck. That's a step down."

"They need to see it as a step forward for the good of the department and the district."

"I suppose this is good news. We're going to be one department again."

"It is good. It'll make your job a lot easier. You'll see. Next year this time, all of you will be thanking Jane."

"I hope you're right."

❖

The following day I went down to the Adult Ed. office to see what I could find out about the planned changes in classrooms and offices. They told me that our department would be in the large area that was serving as two classrooms, a private counseling area, and two small offices. I walked into the huge classroom to try to get a feel for the changes and I could not see them remodeling the area well enough for psychologists, a director, and a secretary.

Since I was feeling a little adventurous, I decided to take Jane up on her word. She had said to me, if I needed anything to let her know. I called her office and was told that she was in and could see me that afternoon. Fate had smiled on me again. This time when I went into Jane's office, it was because I chose to be there, not because she sent for me. Regardless of what happened, I would not have to feel threatened the way I did the last time I was in her office.

Of course I thanked Jane for being willing to see me on such short notice. Then I told her why I had come to see her. “Dr. Smith, I have concerns about the proposed office arrangement for next year. I heard that I will have to move from my current office to one of the Adult Ed. classrooms.”

“Oh, don’t worry about the classrooms. They’ll be gone by the time you get back in August. We’re going to completely remodel the classrooms and turn them into very nice offices for the Special Services Department.”

“That’s great, but I went by the area and I couldn’t see how it would work.”

“I’ll tell you what. Let’s go out there now and we can see what needs to be done.”

“Now?”

“Yes, I’ll drive.”

I had no choice at that point but to ride with Jane in her brand new Cadillac back out to Vo-Teck. She was proud of her new pearl white car. I’m sure the color was listed as something else, but it looked pearl white to me. We were riding in style and comfort, all the way from the D.O. out to Vo-Teck. I called it the country, but it was really on the outskirts of town, about five miles out.

The office staff in Adult Ed. was shocked when I walked in with the superintendent. It was fantastic PR for me. After all, it’s not everyday that Dr. Smith takes time out to come to Vo-Teck to look at office space for a psychologist. We went into the classroom area and she walked around showing me what they had planned for Special Services. It still didn’t feel right. There was not enough space to create offices for four professionals. But, Jane insisted that there would be more than enough space. She told me that the large classroom in the back would be converted to a conference room for the department and that I could have one of the two small offices. Both of those were unacceptable in my opinion.

"Dr. Smith, these two offices are much too small to accommodate my office furniture. My table is probably larger than either one of these offices."

"We can always expand these offices. Which one do you want?"

"They're the same. I don't think it matters."

"Aw, go ahead and choose one."

"Ok, this one nearest the doorway."

"Good. I'll tell the construction supervisor that this one is yours. We'll enlarge this area so that you can get all of your furniture in here. Don't you worry about a thing. We'll take care of it."

"Thank you so much Dr. Smith. You've helped me to feel much better about the move. It seems as if I have to move at least once a year these days. I think that was bothering me … having to move so much."

"I can assure you this will be your last move for a while."

I took Jane at her word. She was so persuasive. I thought that she was telling the truth and that I would get a decent office again. I forgot for a brief period of time about what seemed to be Jane's propensity for lying. I had forgotten what one of the school nurses, who had been in the district for over 20 years, told me during the controversy over Monty Ray Hill that Jane would lie when the truth would serve her better. That was an understatement.

❖

When I returned to work in August, I was not prepared for the problems that I encountered. First of all, the Special Services staff had already moved in – with much attitude. I was right. They did not want to be at Vo-Teck. They saw it for what it was – a step down. Jane had promised that they would be considered district level and would be treated as such even if they were five miles away from the D.O. She convinced them that although physically they would be out at Vo-Teck, on the organizational chart they would still be district personnel. The secretary told me that when they moved out, Jane sent word that they were to take everything from Special Services with them. She didn't want anything from the department left in the administration building – no records, not even a folder. Everything had to go to Vo-Teck. She didn't want anyone to know that Special Services had ever been in the building.

Secondly, and most important, I did not have adequate office space. The maintenance workers had moved most of my furniture into that cubby that they called my office, but some of it was left in the workroom because the office was too small to accommodate everything. The Special Services director had taken my large table without my permission and said that she planned to use it for conferences since it couldn't fit in my office. I explained to her as tactfully as I could that that particular table was a piece of my office furniture and if I managed to move into that cubby, they were going to have to put the table in there as well. That table had been with me from the first move to the basement at the district office and I did not plan to let someone new come into the district and take it at that point.

Fortunately, the maintenance crew was able to manage to get the table into my office. But the situation became a powerful incentive for me to begin my own personal campaign to get a suitable office. This time I was working solo.

CHAPTER 18

The two months between the elections in November and the new school board taking office in January zipped by in what seemed like no time at all. In some cases, time flies whether you're having fun or not. Before we knew it, the time had come for the newly elected board members to replace the old board members who would no longer be serving. By law, the first meeting in January is always held at 10:00 in the morning rather than at night, as is customary. Because of the intense media interest, the meeting was scheduled for the vocational center. The people's board was going to be installed at Vo-Teck. Somehow that seemed most appropriate.

The satellite trucks were back again on that morning in January with reporters from the three TV stations in Columbia. The board meeting was held in the huge auditorium at Vo-Teck which had been used during the peak of the controversial anti-Jane Smith gatherings. It was probably selected because it could easily seat a large turnout without creating any problems for the fire marshal.

I asked for, and received, permission to attend the board meeting since it was scheduled during regular school hours. My video camera battery was fully charged and ready to be used as I recorded the momentous occasion. Louise and I met in her office near the auditorium so that we had a good view of the people as they entered the building.

In spite of all the media attention, the actual attendance was somewhat disappointing. We assumed that after the elections, there was not the same level of concern about the direction that the board would take. Whatever the reason, the audience appeared to consist mainly of family and friends of the new board members.

The main thing that the media had an interest in was the swearing in of the youngest board member, Greg Townsend. The cameras were rolling when he was sworn in so as not to miss any details. There was a segment on all of the local TV stations that evening on the 7:00 and 11:00 p.m. news shows with videos of Greg taking the oath of office. He was interviewed afterwards about being the youngest person ever elected to a school board in the state. Of course, there were the inevitable questions about his role in the Monty Ray Hill protests. For someone so young, Greg handled it well.

The nine board members elected Dewey Fowler as chairman and Mark Graves as vice-chairman after they were all sworn in when they conducted business for the first time. It had been rumored that Dewey and Mark would hold their respective offices, so no one was really surprised. Then the board elected Peter Jones as their chaplain. Celeste was not nominated for any office, which in my opinion was a shame. She had a tremendous amount of experience and knowledge that would serve the board well. Clearly they didn't share my opinion.

The remaining four new board members included Susie Purle, Howard Moore, Connie Scott, and Victor Stone. The last member listed, Victor Stone, was older than Greg Townsend, but he was still young enough to be included on the evening news as one of the youngest board members in the state. So we had three board members from the West Sandhills area: Susie, Howard, and Greg. There were three from the downtown-Lucien Heights area: Celeste, Peter, and Dewey. And the final three were from points north of Lucien Heights all the way to the county line in the north: Mark, Connie, and Victor. The people's board was finally in place.

❖

The question was being asked almost immediately after the first school board meeting of the newly elected members. When are they going to fire Jane Smith? No one knew. In actuality, you can't get elected, get sworn in, and then fire the superintendent after the first couple of board meetings. It simply could not happen. It would have been what the majority of the public wanted, but it could not happen that way. The board members had to learn to function as board members first and foremost. In spite of the campaign promises, there was real work that had to be done. There was a school district that needed the board of trustees to do its job of developing and monitoring policy.

In order to do what needed to be done, the individuals who set policy for the school district would have to go to school themselves. The new board members had to be trained. They had to learn to be board members. It only made common sense, but it was also a state requirement. There was a state school board association in place that did just that – trained new board members. Some of the board members had to learn the basics such as parliamentary procedure. It was new and different for most of them. They also had to learn to work together as a board. They may have all won on a solitary promise, but they had to learn to work as an elected body, not just as elected individuals. Clearly, there was work to be done.

None of this went unnoticed by Jane Smith. Ever resourceful, ever opportunistic, she had the perfect situation for many months to promote her own agenda and make herself look good while making the board look bad. One of the things that she did was to stretch the meetings out. Her agendas were chock full of all kinds of items that were guaranteed to challenge even the most experienced board member. The marathon meetings began with the second meeting in January and became standard fare for the board.

There was something almost sinister in the way the marathon meetings began shaping the public's perception of the board. When board meetings that used to begin at 7 and end before 11 started lasting until 2 and 3 o'clock in the morning, there was definitely something wrong.

❖

I didn't realize how bad the situation was becoming with the marathon meetings until I ran into one of Jane's supporters at Academy Street Elementary School. This was the school where the male principal was replaced by a female because Jane felt the children needed a woman running things. The teacher approached me in the hallway and asked me if I had heard the latest about the "ignorant board". She caught me completely off guard with her question. At first I thought she was joking, but one look at her expression told me that she was quite serious.

"Ignorant board?" I asked.

She replied indignantly, "Yes, most of them are too ignorant to be on the board."

"What makes you say that?"

"I heard from Dr. Smith that they don't understand anything about procedures and they keep tying her up, asking stupid questions. She can't get home until the middle of the night."

"The middle of the night? How late are you talking about?"

"I heard way past one o'clock – sometimes as late as three o'clock and even later."

"What? Three o'clock in the morning? What on earth could they be doing that late at night?"

"That's just it, they don't know what they're doing so they keep Dr. Smith there trying to educate them on how to do their jobs."

"That doesn't make any sense. This is the first that I've heard about any of this. I really don't know what's going on, but I can tell you one thing for sure, I'll find out."

"Well I'm telling you. I got it from Jane's sister. She works downtown with a friend of mine. She said it's terrible. Poor Jane is too tired the next day to go to work, but she has no choice. It's taking its toll on her. Poor thing."

"No, I'm going to ask some people on the board what is going on. I'll call Celeste if necessary. If what you're saying is true, that doesn't make any sense at all."

"It's true. Trust me. Celeste will tell you the same thing."

I was stunned. I had never heard anyone speak so disparagingly about a school board before in my life. I knew that there were times when someone might disagree with the board, but to call them ignorant. That was unheard of. I thought there had to be an explanation for what was happening. Surely the board wouldn't spend half the night asking questions. And, if board members did have questions, why would Jane be the person to answer them? They had other resources available. They could consult the school board attorney or the representative from the school board association. Something was not right with what I had just been told.

I called Stacy that evening to explain to her what had been described to me and also to find out what Mark was saying about the board meetings. The first thing I wanted to do was to find out about the marathon meetings, to learn whether or not they were meeting until all hours of the night.

So when I called, that was my first question: "Stacy, has the board been having marathon meetings?"

"Well hello to you too Claire," That was her way of reminding me that I hadn't said bothered to say hello. Then she laughed and said, "You must really be upset about something. What kind of marathon meetings?"

"I am upset by what I heard today. I call them marathon meetings because I was told the board has been meeting non-stop from 7 p.m. until two and three o'clock in the morning."

"They have been getting home late. I know Mark has been. I was worried the first time it happened and stayed up until he got home, but now I've been able to go to bed."

"Why are they meeting so late? I don't believe I've ever heard of a board routinely meeting so late."

"They shouldn't, but Mark says that Jane ties them up with unbelievably long agendas."

"It's making the board look bad. People think they're staying late because the board is asking her questions. She claims she's doing on the job training."

"That's not true. Where is that coming from?"

"From Jane. She's saying all of that."

"Why am I not surprised?" Stacy sounded disgusted, "I'm going to discuss it with Mark later when he gets in. He needs to know what Jane is telling the public."

I agreed, but I wanted everyone to know. So I told her, "They all need to know, Stacy … the entire board."

She agreed, "You're right, they do need to know, but what can they do?"

"Who sets the agenda?" I asked. "It seems to me I remember that when Celeste was chairing the board, she met with the superintendent to plan the agenda."

"I think you're right," Stacy said. Then she answered my question, "I believe Dewey meets with Jane."

I pointed out, "If that's the case, he can do something about the length of the agenda. Some things can be scheduled for a later time or they can even schedule another meeting, a special called meeting, if necessary."

"That's true. Let me talk with Mark and I'll let you know what he says, Ok?"

"That's fine," I said.

When Stacy got back with me, she was furious. She told me the situation was worse than she thought. The board members felt that Jane Smith was trying to wear them down. It was not just that the agendas were lengthy; it was that the majority of items on the agenda should not have been brought before the board. Jane was asking them to micromanage and then complaining about them being ignorant. After Stacy told Mark what was being said publicly about the board, he discussed it with Dewey. Then Dewey put it on the agenda to be reviewed by the full board in executive session.

Following a lengthy review of lengthy agendas in a lengthy executive session, the board voted in open session to bring in a consultant from the state school board association to meet with the board and the superintendent. Now it was Jane Smith who was furious. Once the consultant from the school board association came to Dane County and discussed the situation with Jane and with the board, the marathon meetings decreased significantly. Interesting how the board went from being ignorant to knowledgeable just by bringing in a consultant.

❖

The board members took their newfound expertise a step further and formed committees to inspect the two newly completed high schools. It was understood that any of the board members could visit both of the schools and check them out, but the committee members had a responsibility to actually examine their assigned schools and talk with the administrators and staff from the maintenance department about the quality of the construction and building operations.

It turned out to be a learning experience of a lifetime for the committee members. There were reportedly so many problems with the schools that the members who were employed ended up having to take time off from their jobs to be able to handle the inspections. One of the members, Connie Scott told me during a phone conversation that it was requiring more time than anyone had anticipated.

I wasn't familiar with the specifics of their committee work and asked, "What exactly are you doing in the schools?"

"It's not both schools. Some of us have Lucien Heights and some of the board members are assigned to Riverplains High."

I wanted to be certain that I understood her, so I asked, "What you're saying is that you have only Lucien Heights, but that is requiring a lot of your time?"

"Exactly," she replied. "What started out to be a fairly simple proposal for some of us to visit each new high school and make sure that everything is in order had turned out to be a real boondoggle."

"How so?"

"The district hired private supervisors and the construction company had their own supervisors so technically there should not have been any major problems with either one of the facilities."

"But that's not the case?" I asked.

Connie had the tone of frustration in her voice when she explained, "No, we're finding that there are major problems with both schools. Some of it has to do with shoddy materials and some has to do with what appear to be design flaws."

"Design flaws?" This was interesting.

"Uh-huh. A good example is the skylight in the cafeteria at Riverplains High and there is no air conditioning."

That made no sense. "No air conditioning and we're in South Carolina?"

Connie agreed, "Yup. That's what I meant. The skylight lets in heat and then you have heat from the ovens added to the area and the place is unbearable."

"I'm sure it is. In August the afternoon temperature is in the 90's."

Connie continued to share her own personal frustration and that of the board with me. "That means we've got to hire another firm to correct the problems. It's the same kind of thing at Lucien Heights. Not heat in the cafeteria, but water problems with the plumbing. It has to do with the placement of the pipes."

"It sounds like you do have your work cut out for you." I could tell she was put out with the situation and their inherited responsibilities.

"This is not even my job, but we have to do it if it's going to be done."

I couldn't help but wonder if the current board members had talked with some of the former members. Celeste was still on the board. Surely they questioned her. "Did you ask Celeste about the firms that they hired?"

"She made a comment about Dane County not being a wealthy district and what did you expect for the money."

"No she didn't!"

"Oh yes. I asked her how she would feel if she was walking down the hall at Lucien Heights High and the floor gave way."

"What'd she say?"

"Told me you couldn't expect top of the line facilities with bargain basement money or something like that."

I laughed, "Celeste has such a great sense of humor."

"I didn't think it was funny. She won't even serve on any of the committees to go into the schools to see what the problems are."

I suspected that Celeste felt left out of some of the private discussions mainly because she was still viewed as loyal to Jane Smith. I said to Connie, "She may just feel that the board doesn't include her in other matters and so she'll let you handle this on your own."

"We try to include her but she's so negative."

"But she's also knowledgeable and experienced."

Connie's tone was uncharacteristically harsh. "Then she should put some of her knowledge and experience to use in helping to get these facilities straightened out."

"Who knows, in time there may be a more harmonious relationship between all of the board members."

"You're right, but for now we have to use the help that we have from people who are willing to work together to get the job done."

❖

There was considerable concern over the decline in attendance at the board meetings. There were significantly fewer people attending board meetings after the first month. The numbers continued to decline until it seemed as if no one really cared about what was going on anymore with the board. On the face of it, either the county residents had reverted back to pre-Monty Ray apathy or there was trust among the voters that the board would do the right thing, whatever that was. And, to be perfectly honest, I was not going to board meetings any longer, nor were my friends, Louise and Stacy. Regardless of the reasons, the meetings were sparsely attended for the most part. In light of that, and to give each area of the county a chance to easily attend the meetings, the board decided to change the location of the meetings during the school year and meet in a different school on the first and third Tuesdays.

Meeting in the schools within the district gave each school a chance to feature a School Spotlight at the beginning of the meetings. Attendance problems quickly became a thing of the past. This was because the School Spotlight typically showcased students making presentations or performing for the board. As the board realized, parents would definitely be in attendance if their children were going to be a part of the evening's agenda. It worked. After the 'traveling school board' took their show on the road, the meetings were always well attended. People had to come early to get a seat because the room where the meeting was held would fill up quickly. However, after the School Spotlight, you could sit virtually anyplace that you wanted to because once the parents left with their children, the audience shrank noticeably.

CHAPTER 19

The board members were actually quick learners, and on the surface it almost appeared to be business as usual, just with a different board. There was, however, an undercurrent of anticipation. There was still the expectation that something was going to be done about Dr. Jane Smith. People didn't know what, but they expected that something would be done before too long. But, they didn't want to have to wait for too long. So it wasn't surprising when people started to question board members about when they planned to fire Jane Smith.

Stacy, Louise, and I talked a lot at Vo-Teck over the next several weeks after the new board was installed. We all felt that the main issue facing the board was that of taking action against Dr. Smith on behalf of the people of the county. We recognized that we needed to seriously address the fact that we had reservations about the board attorney and his loyalty to the school board versus his loyalty to Jane Smith. Even though the attorney was supposed to represent the board, lots of times it appeared that the attorney was representing the superintendent. That was because the superintendent and the board generally worked so closely together.

It was easy to understand how people sometimes forgot that if the board hired the attorney, it was the board's attorney and not the superintendent's attorney. That's why board members called him 'their' legal counsel. He was the school board's attorney and not Dr. Jane Smith's attorney. We needed to consider too, that although the legal advice from the attorney was presented to the superintendent and to the board, it was given as a legal opinion regarding what would be in the best interest of the district – meaning the board. At any rate, the distinction as to representation by the attorney was so unclear in most people's minds that it was no wonder that the public and the superintendent thought the board attorney was her attorney.

❖

Instead of meeting during brief breaks at Vo-Teck and calling each other in the evening, Stacy thought that the three of us should get together for a serious meeting about the board members. We hadn't done that in a long time, not seriously since the elections. She felt that it was time for us to look carefully at each board member and then develop strategies for achieving our goal of bringing new leadership into the county for the school district. Louise and I were willing to meet as soon as possible so we scheduled a meeting for Saturday morning at Louise's house. It was always easier to meet at Louise's because we had the privacy we needed and her house was centrally located.

On a Saturday morning the three of us sat at Louise's dining room table and began by looking at board members individually.

Stacy mentioned that Mark was still very much committed to firing Jane Smith. She went on to say, "If Mark could fire her by himself, he would do it."

Louise nodded in agreement and stated, "I believe that he is and I also think Susie Purle is strongly committed to getting a new superintendent."

Stacy commented, "Susie listens to Mark. They have become very close over the past few weeks. The whole board is close, but Susie seems to respect Mark and listen to what he has to say."

I asked, "In board meetings?"

"No, in and out of board meetings. She calls Mark a lot in the evening to ask his opinion about the schools or board matters."

"I don't think we have to worry about Susie Purle", Louise said in a very matter of fact tone. "She made her position known long before the election. Isn't that what you said Claire?"

"Yes," I replied. "Susie planned to run for the school board back when she was still working as a secretary at the elementary school in Riverplains. She said then that something needed to be done about Jane. She had decided to run for the school board even before single member districts and her goal was always to get rid of Jane Smith."

Stacy stated what we all knew. "So Mark and Susie are two that we know will support firing Jane if it comes to a vote."

But Louise wanted more information on Stacy's friend, Connie. She asked, "Stacy, can we depend on Connie to vote to fire Jane?"

"Oh, absolutely, without any hesitation. She despises the woman. Sometimes I wonder if it's not personal between them. Connie cannot stand Jane Smith!"

"Good." Louise was satisfied so she moved on to the next board member, "What do you know about Dewey Fowler? Can we trust him?"

Stacy had some information. "I do know that he and Connie are very close. They talk all the time. I don't think Dewey was as strong in support of firing Jane as some of the board members when he campaigned, but I think as chairman, he will support the majority decision."

"He's a member of that downtown clique, he'll vote to fire Jane. They never wanted her to become superintendent. They just tolerate her now. Old Dewey will do the right thing. He's got to live with his constituents." Louise's comments were said with that slow deliberate way she had of talking when she was serious. We all started laughing.

I ventured my opinion that, "Greg Townsend will surely vote to fire Jane. He's a lot like Susie Purle; he wanted to get rid of her long before he got on the board. The board seat is a means to an end."

Stacy agreed, "Yeah. We don't have to be worried about Greg. He'll add his vote to terminate Jane. I think that the whole Riverplains group will vote to fire her. That includes Howard Moore."

At the mention of Howard's name, I asked, "He rarely says anything in the board meetings. It's kind of hard to know where he stands. I know he generally votes with the majority, but do you really think that he will do that with something as important as firing a superintendent?"

"Oh yeah. Howard doesn't say much because he's not comfortable speaking in public, but he can't stand Jane. He'd like to fire her today," Stacy said with assurance.

I summarized, "We've got Susie Purle, Howard Moore, and Greg Townsend from the Riverplains area all strongly in support of terminating Jane. Then on this side of the river, we have the chairman, Dewey Fowler, the vice-chairman, Mark, and then finally, we have Connie Scott. That's six. We have a clear majority. All we need is five, but we've got one to spare."

"We need to make it unanimous," Louise stressed.

"Why?" I asked.

"Anytime you have a major decision like this, it needs to be unanimous. The entire board needs to be in support of it."

I replied, "But we'll never get Celeste to vote against Jane. She's defended her far too long and they're such good friends."

Louise countered, "I didn't say it would be unanimous, I just said it needs to be unanimous. We can try to get Celeste to go along with the rest of the board or we can let the vote be 8-1 with Celeste being the only one against it."

"Oh, I don't know about Peter Jones. He has been working closely with Celeste and someone said they thought Junior and Jane had invited him to dinner." Stacy smiled as she told us about the Smiths and Peter Jones.

Louise was clearly put out by the Smiths. "It's good to know that some things and some people never change. It's just like Junior and Jane to snow Peter Jones by banking on their reputation in the black community."

Stacy suggested, "Claire, you might be able to talk with Peter. He'd listen to you. You and Celeste are friends, so he would respect your opinion."

I asked, "Me? You want me to talk to Peter Jones?"

"Why not?" Louise was now questioning me.

I replied, "I don't know him. I have to build some type of rapport before I approach him about firing Jane. I mean, I can't just call him up and say that he needs to vote to fire Jane."

Stacy responded by saying, "I think that you're the best person. You can call him about something else and get to the firing later, after you feel comfortable talking with him. You could probably get to the firing in about three calls or so."

Louise and I both laughed. Louise said, "Now we know how you handle men Stacy. You move quickly."

Stacy didn't see the humor. "No, this is totally different. Claire's going to handle this the way she does any project to help the community. She's not going after him personally, just his vote."

"Ah, flattery will win every time," I said and laughed again. "I'll start getting to know Peter just a little better ladies."

We ended up moving on to other topics at that point and completely forgot about Victor Stone. He was the representative on the board from the northernmost area of the county in the Cedar Hills area. We didn't know much about him and it was hard to predict how he would vote. The only thing that we knew with certainty was that he didn't like to be the odd man out. So when push came to shove, he'd more than likely be on the side of the majority. And coming from Cedar Hills he couldn't end up being the only board member on Celeste's side. He wouldn't be able to go home that night if he voted with Celeste against his fellow board members. That wasn't going to happen.

CHAPTER 20

Following our strategy session at Louise's house, I asked my mother about a friend of hers who had experience on a school board in a neighboring county. Her friend, Betty Logan, had been chairman of her county school board for eight years and had been a member of the board for twice as long. The main reason that I wanted to talk with the lady was because I knew from the *Carolina* newspaper and the evening news on TV that her school board did not hesitate to fire superintendents. They had a reputation of firing more superintendents than any of the surrounding counties. Dane County, for example, had never fired a superintendent.

When I called Ms. Logan, I introduced myself as the daughter of Mildred Christianson. She said that she remembered me from when I much younger because of her involvement with my mother through the Presbyterian Church and had tried to keep up with me over the years. She wanted to know if I was still a school psychologist.

I replied, "Yes, ma'am. I'm still a psychologist. I'm in Dane County now."

She was clearly familiar with Dane County by her next question: "Have things settled down over there with Dr. Jane Smith?"

"Not exactly. That's why I'm calling. I need your advice."

"I'll be glad to help you if I can," she said. Then she asked, "What's going on?"

"Dr. Smith had been trying to make the board look bad by filling up the agenda with administrative issues and then keeping them late in meetings. But I think that those problems have been resolved."

"Good. I'm glad to hear that."

I was encouraged to continue, "What I need advice on now is a good school board attorney. I know that your district has not had a problem terminating superintendents and I wanted to know who your school board attorney is."

She did not hesitate in responding, "Oh, Marvin Younkins. Marvin is one of the best school board attorneys in the state. His firm represents a large number of school districts."

"Marvin Younkins. Is he from Columbia?"

"Yes, his law firm is in Columbia, but he travels all over the state on behalf of school districts," she stated with the assurance of someone who knew what they were talking about.

He sounded perfect for Dane County. So I told her, "We need someone who will help the board fire Jane Smith."

"Honey, Marvin is your man. He is brilliant. He knows school law inside out. You won't have any problems if he is representing your board."

"That's the kind of person we need. Someone from out of town who can come in and advise the board on the best way to handle Jane Smith."

"Who do you have now?" she asked.

"You probably don't know him, he's a local attorney. Some of us feel that he will not be the attorney to handle the legal aspect of terminating the superintendent. He's too close to the situation and he's caught up in local politics."

"Let me give you Marvin's number and you can have one of the board members call him and talk with him so that they can form their own opinion."

"Thanks."

"Marvin is not only a fantastic attorney, he is a good Christian and he has high ethical standards."

"Isn't that an oxymoron?"

"What is?"

"Ethical attorney." Then I realized that I didn't need to go in that direction. So I said. "Ms. Logan, I was just joking. But if he has high ethical standards and is a good Christian, I think some of the board members will love him."

"Oh great. Here's the number."

❖

In the interest of expediency, I called Mark Graves that same night, since he was the vice-chairman and a good friend, to lay the groundwork for bringing in another attorney. He was receptive to the idea of a Christian attorney with high ethical standards representing the board. I stressed that this attorney, Marvin Younkins, was one of the most experienced school board attorneys in the state in the area of terminating superintendents. It seemed appropriate also to remind Mark of the promise that he and the other board members had made when they were campaigning – to do something about Jane Smith, even if it meant firing her. Mark understood and confirmed that he was still committed, but from a practical standpoint, he wanted to point out to me that his vote was just one of nine. He went on to say that I would probably want to talk with some of the other board members about retaining Mr. Younkins if we were going to be successful. I readily agreed.

I didn't talk to Louise about the attorney, because it didn't seem to be an issue that she would be interested in pursuing. I knew that she had a good working relationship with the current school board attorney and there was always the potential for a conflict of interest. So, I decided to let her learn about the new attorney when, and if, the board hired him.

Once I had spoken with Mark Graves, the next person that I needed to contact about Marvin Younkins was Connie Scott. Because Connie, Mark, and Stacy were such good friends, convincing one of them would make it easier to convince all of them. Connie and I had become good friends following the celebration dinner in Columbia and I found out quickly that my assessment about her sense of humor was quite accurate. She could be really funny at times. She was an astute judge of character and knew things about people in the county that I would never have imagined. There was probably a difference of 10 years in our ages, with Connie being younger, but she had the wisdom of someone much older.

When I called Connie, I explained that I had some reservations about the current school board attorney. "I think that if the board decided to follow-through with the campaign promises and move in the direction of terminating Jane, the board attorney might be resistant."

"Why do you think that?" Connie asked with genuine concern.

"There may be a problem with Jane's interests versus the board's interests. I'm not sure that this attorney will be loyal to the board. He may feel compelled to protect Jane's interests and not look at what will be best for the county."

"Oh, I don't know. He seems pretty sharp."

"I have to tell you, Connie, I disagree. Remember, he was the one who allowed the board to vote in executive session for the shared principal plan and never cautioned them in open session. Sometimes I think he will allow Jane to do whatever she wants to and not advise the board otherwise."

"I had forgotten about the share-a-principal fiasco with the old board, but we haven't had any problems with him since I've been on the board."

"Have you had to ask him for a legal opinion about anything ... one of Jane's proposals or anything?"

"Not really."

"So you don't know much about his legal competence or where his loyalty lies."

"I guess not. I hadn't thought about like that before. He just seems like an affable man."

"Uh-huh. He presents himself as the Lucien Heights version of Ben Matlock. That'll hold up probably until you disagree with Jane. It'll be interesting to see how he handles himself then."

"Do you think we need to talk with him specifically about his responsibilities?"

"Actually, I was hoping you might be interested in talking with another attorney, Marvin Younkins. This man specializes in school law. Your current attorney is a part-time school board attorney and a full-time ambulance chaser."

"You're suggesting that we hire an attorney who specializes in school law?"

I laughed, "Now that's a novel idea – a school board hiring an attorney who specializes in school law. Actually what I'd like to suggest is that you talk with Marvin Younkins yourself and then form your own opinion. He represents a large number of school districts in the state and has extensive experience in dealing with superintendents like Dr. Smith."

"Oh, you know him personally?"

"No, but I spoke recently with someone who has known him for many years as a friend and as a board attorney. The woman that I spoke with is a board chairman in another county and is my mother's long-time friend. Her name is Betty Logan and she was full of nothing but praise concerning Marvin Younkins. She's been keeping up with the school district here in Dane County and she thinks that Mr. Younkins might be just what we need. He might be able to help us out."

"Interesting. But, even if I talk with this attorney, Mr. Younkins, I can't make a decision by myself. You know that."

"Yes, I'm well aware of that. Mark told me the same thing. I talked with him a few nights ago and he sounded receptive to the idea of at least contacting Marvin. My feeling is that you need to have the right attorney representing the board if you are going to be able to find a way to terminate Jane Smith without facing a multimillion dollar lawsuit or worse."

"You're right about that. We don't know enough about school law to be able to make sound decisions about Jane at this point. Mark may be right. We probably need to at least contact Marvin Younkins and find out about his services."

I laughed again and said, "It just so happens I have his phone number … courtesy of Betty Logan."

Connie laughed too and then proceeded to write down the number as I gave it to her.

❖

The more things change …

The next board meeting was less than a week away. I hadn't been attending the meetings as faithfully as I had during the controversial period, but if I was now putting myself in the position of advising the board on hiring an attorney, it would be a good idea for me to have first hand knowledge of the board's current status. I was going to have to go alone because my sons were definitely not interested in going. Christian was never interested and that had not changed. Michael was bored the last time couple of times he went with me after the new board was installed and things settled down. He was so considerate though; he gave me some advice when I asked him about accompanying me once again.

"Mom, I think you'll be alright if you make sure you have your mace or pepper spray with you."

"So you won't come to the meetings with me the way you used to?"

"No, I don't think you have anything to worry about now," he said with a smile. "Oh, and get someone to walk with you to your car when you're getting ready to come home."

I had to laugh because he was so serious, but I had to let him know that I appreciated his suggestions, "Thanks for the safety and security tips."

My decision to resume attending the board meetings coincided with the time that Stacy was investigating various types of car phones. She found a good model from a local dealer in Lucien Heights and recommended that I might want to get a car phone too since I was often out at night at school board meetings. I followed-up immediately on her recommendation. The model that I bought was called transportable and the phone was in a bag. There was a rechargeable battery which allowed me to use it away from the car. It was so cumbersome compared to the phones that came out later, but it was great for giving me a sense of security when I had to attend board meetings at night. And it really came in handy when I had to go to the outlying areas.

❖

The school board meetings were being held all over the county because of the board's insistence on meeting in every single school in the district. It took some time for the public to become accustomed to the traveling school board. For as long as anyone could remember, the meetings had always been held in the boardroom at the administration building or in a nearby school when the attendance numbers were high. But, unless you called the school district or checked the newspaper, there was no way to know which school would be hosting the meeting. I remember one man, who spoke during the public forum, said that it had taken him forever that evening to find the meeting. He told the board, "You guys are harder to find than a floating craps game."

When I started back attending the meetings, it was readily apparent that the board members had learned a great deal more about procedures. There were a few missteps from time to time, but these were usually due to a lack of guidance from the legal advisor rather than anything the board members had done. One striking example was the night the board was preparing to vote on an administrative position for one of the high schools and someone made a comment about getting all the facts out in the open. So they consulted the board attorney who told them it was fine to discuss everything about the candidates in open session. It was not. The particular discussion being questioned would have involved personnel matters and as such it would have to be conducted in executive session. The attorney should have been knowledgeable of that. It's a part of School Board Basics 101. Fortunately several of the board members understood the distinction and overruled the attorney's advice.

❖

One good thing that came out my attendance at the board meetings was that I had an opportunity to get to know more about Peter Jones and to build a friendship with him. It was apparent early on that he and Celeste had bonded and were closely aligned. The two of them usually voted together even if it meant that their votes were the only ones in opposition to a motion. The board was frequently divided 7-2. That was not a good thing because it was divided along racial lines. Peter and Celeste would often support proposals from other board members, but that support was rarely, if ever, reciprocated. The other board members had formed the opinion that Celeste was so loyal to Jane Smith that they never gave her a chance as a board member. They just turned a deaf ear to her motions and comments. There was not an attempt to learn from her or to utilize her expertise.

Peter and I chatted occasionally during the brief breaks or before the meetings began. Sometimes Celeste would join us. I did not want to be seen as singling Peter out so I often conversed with the other board members, especially my friends Connie and Mark. My impression was that the board members were willing to treat Peter differently from Celeste, but they rarely had an opportunity to demonstrate that. He had a good rapport with the most of the other board members and would have been a part of everything that they were involved in, but he chose to support Celeste. I wondered if that was because he agreed with her or if it was perhaps so that she would not feel alone on the board.

Eventually I felt comfortable enough with Peter to ask him how he felt about terminating Jane Smith. He was taken aback by my question and had some difficulty responding. He managed to say, "I don't have a problem with Dr. Smith as a superintendent. I think that the board needs to keep an open mind in dealing with her."

"I'm sure you're right, but the relationship between Dr. Smith and the board is strained, to say the least."

Peter came to her defense immediately. "That's not all her fault. I blame some of the board members. They're not willing to listen to her and give her a chance."

I pressed on, "You know she has trouble with the truth. You've seen that with some issues that have come before the board. She's told you one thing and then you later get factual information that directly contradicts what she has said."

Still defensive, he said, "That has happened, but I don't see that as an ongoing problem."

"Peter, I know that some people voted for you because they didn't trust your opponent, Jessie Taylor, to vote against Jane if necessary. They saw Jessie as part of the old guard that would support Jane no matter what."

"Is that true? I think most black people support Jane anyway. I don't see how they would choose me or Jessie just because of that."

"You say that now, but the issue of firing Jane Smith was foremost in everyone's mind during the campaign." Then I reminded him, "And, you don't have just blacks in your district anyway."

He chuckled, "You're right about that I do have a sizable white constituency."

"I know because some of them have said to me that they would never have voted for Jessie. On the other hand, they liked you because you seemed to know what the public wanted."

"That's true."

"Some of them are staunch, die-hard conservative Republicans who supported you … and still are supporting you."

He conceded, "Yeah, I do have a lot of Republican support."

"Well think about it, Junior is a lifelong Democrat and so is Jane, What do you think the conservatives expect you to do?"

"They're just going to have to trust my judgment."

"I'm sure they will. They'll trust you to support the board when the vote comes to terminate Jane," I asserted with a smile.

Peter smiled too and said, "I'll vote my convictions when the time comes … if that time comes."

❖

When we had that conversation, it was just one of many that we had together before the board made a decision as whether or not Marvin Younkins would be retained. The conversations with Peter then, were almost in preparation for some future time when a vote might be taken.

Finally, that 'future' time was beginning to look like a real possibility before too long because Connie and Mark had spoken with Marvin and were very impressed. They were the ones who had the responsibility of getting Dewey to meet with him and then hopefully take the matter before the entire board.

Things were moving along smoothly. Surprisingly all was well, extremely well, in the school board attorney arena. I found this out when Connie called me less than a month after I had approached her about Marvin Younkins to tell me that the board had made a major decision.

"I hope the decision was favorable to my position."

"It's better than that. It was favorable to the board's position," she laughingly corrected me.

"So tell me! Tell me quickly before I explode with curiosity!"

"You may explode with joy when I tell you what we're going to do."

"As long as you get rid of the attorney you currently have for Marvin Younkins, I'll be fine. I'll try to limit my explosions to tiny ones – mini explosions." Then I laughed because by this time Connie's humorous spirit had done its work. I was infected too. My spirits were so high.

"If you had come to the last board meeting you would know and you would've been dancing around last Tuesday night instead of tonight."

"You mean you fired one attorney and hired another?"

"Not exactly. We tried to go for a satisfactory and workable compromise."

"Which was?"

"It was a decision to keep the local attorney for routine board matters, but to hire Marvin Younkins for special projects."

"Yes! Yes! Yes! And those special projects include firing controversial superintendents, I'm sure."

"Of course. I knew you'd be pleased."

"To say the least! We're making history! We finally have a reputable school board attorney representing Dane County school district." By this time Connie and I both were laughing over this turn of events. My enthusiasm continued unabated.

"I'm so excited! This is the best news I've heard coming out of that board in a long time."

"We're going to have a special, called meeting Thursday night to meet with Marvin Younkins. This meeting will be just for the board members and Younkins. The superintendent will not be allowed."

"I love it when a plan comes together."

"You and me both!"

When I hung up the phone, I immediately went to find my mother so that I could tell her what Connie said.

CHAPTER 21

Some things never change …

The problems continued with my office space or lack thereof. I complained whenever I had the chance about how the district was treating professionals by not giving us adequate workspace. Louise's husband, Al, checked the fire code for our building and suggested that I get the county fire marshal to come out to Vo-Teck and look for violations. He suspected that the school district was in violation of numerous requirements and aspects of the fire code.

The truth of the matter was that I had problems on a more basic level – just in meeting with someone in my office. The only way for a visitor, such as a parent, to sit in my office would be for that person to block the doorway. That was unacceptable. The room that I was in was never meant to be a private office as best I could tell. It was designed to be a records area with only enough space for a small desk and chair. It was located between two classrooms and there were doors on either side of the small, rectangular area. The doors permitted the previous occupants to walk through easily from one classroom to another.

As luck would have it, Mark Graves came to do an on-site visit of Vo-Teck to talk with employees and get feedback on their working conditions. When Stacy mentioned to me that he would be at Vo-Teck, I asked her to bring him by my office. I said it wouldn't hurt for a board member to see what I had to contend with and how Jane had forced me to work in an unsuitable area. Mark graciously agreed to check out my office while he was touring Vo-Teck. He came, looked around, and started laughing.

I recall asking, "Why are you laughing Mark? What is so funny?"

He replied, as he continued to laugh, "A hot dog stand."

"A hot dog stand?"

"Yeah, a hot dog stand."

"What about a hot dog stand?"

"That's what your office reminds me of – a hot dog stand."

By this time, Stacy started laughing too. As they left, Mark was still laughing and shaking his head. I smiled, but I never laughed because I could not forget that it was I who had to work in that hot dog stand. From that time on, whenever I mentioned my office problems to anyone, all I had to say was it reminded Mark of a hot dog stand and people understood without any problem. I got tons of much needed sympathy.

❖

In the schools …

Everyone in the entire school district knew about Dr. Smith moving the psychologists from the administration building to the vocational center. It was a pleasant surprise to learn that the reaction in the schools was overwhelmingly positive in favor of us, the psychologists. Ashley resigned to avoid humiliation, but there wasn't any. By virtue of our being victims of Jane Smith's retaliation for not supporting her becoming superintendent, we achieved something akin to martyr status district wide. It was interesting to see that people were taking our side against Jane who had never had even a kind word to say about us in the past.

There were so many examples of teachers and district staff expressing support. One teacher, who had disagreed with me in the past about children that she wanted to refer, now was taking the position that Jane was mean spirited to separate the psychologists from Special Services and to move us out of the district office. It was heartwarming to hear from employees that they were aware of what had happened and wanted me to know that they supported us.

A teacher spoke with me in the office at Academy Street Elementary and said, "I heard about what Dr. Smith did to the psychologists. I just want you to know that a lot of the teachers were talking about it and we think that what she did was unfair."

Another teacher in the same school said, "Dr. Franklin, I am so sorry about what happened to you and the other psychologists."

A fairly common theme was that "The psychologists are district level personnel. You should be at the D.O. Dr. Smith was wrong to send you out to Vo-Teck."

Only one teacher had anything supportive to say about the psychologists being moved by Jane Smith. The woman was an African-American whose husband and Junior Smith were close political allies. She stopped me in the hall at Academy Street and laughed loudly before stating, "I heard that Dr. Smith kicked the psychologists out of the district office. Ha-ha! She showed y'all who's in charge. Ha-ha!"

I did not try to explain anything to that particular teacher. Rather, my response to her was more in reference to the fact that she found it so amusing. I don't believe she heard anything that I was saying. She was too busy laughing. This woman, though, was the exception. Her comments suggested that she had undoubtedly talked about the move with her husband, who in turn had probably already discussed it with his political ally, Junior Smith.

❖

That Junior would brag to that woman's husband about his wife 'showing the psychologist who was in charge', was completely contradictory to what he said to me in confidence after Jane was named superintendent. I happened to be at Broadwater Elementary doing evaluations and I saw Junior as I was letting the office know that I was leaving.

Junior came up to me and asked if I would come in his office for a few minutes. "Dr. Franklin, I just need to speak with you briefly."

"Sure, Mr. Smith. I have time."

"I know you heard that I'll be retiring since Jane is the superintendent."

"Yes, I did."

"Now you know I have always looked out for you whenever Jane tried to move you, I always asked her to let you stay here with me."

I knew that he was telling the truth because he advocated for me to be able to stay in his school more than once and Jane relented each time. "Yes sir, I know that."

"Well, what I want to tell you is that Jane is her own person. She doesn't always listen to me."

"I believe that."

"Well, you should 'cause it's the truth. I can tell her the way I think she ought to do something, but she won't listen to me all the time. Sometimes she'll go ahead and do what I told her I didn't think she should do."

"I understand."

"I want to make sure that you do understand that lots of times she'll do things that I don't agree with."

"I think that's true of almost any married couple."

"Yes it is, but Jane is in a position now to do good for a lot of people."

"Is that right?"

"Oh yeah. People got mad about the shared principal thing, but Jane was trying to save jobs. She was trying to keep people from losing their jobs."

"I didn't know that."

"Very few people knew that. They thought she was trying to take something away from them, but she was trying to help them hold on to the people they had."

"I never knew."

Junior leaned over his desk and lowered his voice as if confiding. "And let me tell you something else. I told Jane I don't trust that downtown crowd she's trying to win over. You can't please that crowd. They don't do anything but keep confusion in town over those elementary schools."

"You're right about that."

"I know I am. You know they don't want but so many black children in those schools. That's why we had to go and rezone all of those schools. All because of that one group of people that think they're better than everybody else."

"I knew about the rezoning. I think most people knew what that was about."

"Jane had to fight for minorities with that rezoning."

I was not convinced. "She did?"

"Yes she did. You'd be surprised how much Jane has tried to help minorities in Dane County."

"I suppose I would."

"Well, I'm not going to keep you, but I wanted to tell you that I talked with Jane. I told her not to surround herself with 'yes-men'. I told her to put someone like you up there with her administration. I know that even if you disagree with her, you'll tell her what you think is in her best interest. Those other folk won't do that."

By this time, I was beginning to get caught up in what Junior was saying. I was becoming a little emotional and I didn't want my eyes to mist up after he made those last comments about recommending me to Jane. Thank goodness he was ending the conversation and I had a chance to leave before he found out that he was getting to me.

"Thank you Mr. Smith."

"You're welcome and if there's ever anything I can do for you, don't hesitate to let me know."

❖

The situation surrounding my lack of adequate and appropriate office space helped to generate yet another controversy. I found out about it from a phone call that I received from the president of the local chapter of the NAACP, Gerald Givens. Gerald called one evening and talked with my mother for a few minutes then asked to speak with me.

I couldn't imagine why he wanted to talk with me, but I took the call without question, "Hi Gerald, how are you? I'm surprised that you want to talk with me instead of my mother."

"I know. Normally when I call it is to speak with your mother, but tonight I need to discuss something with you."

"No problem."

Gerald lowered his voice. "I spoke with Dr. Jane Smith earlier this evening."

"Oh my goodness. Not another Jane-related horror story."

"You might want to call it that after I tell you what happened. When I called her I explained that I was concerned about your office space at Vo-Teck."

"I know you didn't! What did she have to say?"

His voice became higher and more excited. "She shocked me. I'm still trying to process everything that she said."

"What on earth did she say to you?"

"She told me that you were a thorn in her side."

By this time I raised my voice and asked, "Me, a thorn in HER side?"

In his crisp business tone he commented, "That was precisely my question to her." He continued, "She said that she had put you in her car and taken you to Vo-Teck to look at office space and that you selected your office and told her that you were satisfied."

"Oh, Gerald. I know she didn't tell you that. Why she's not telling the truth."

He said softly, "It gets better, or worse depending on your perspective."

"Go on."

"She asked me if you had come to me for help. I told her no that you were not aware that I was going to call her. I could tell she didn't believe me, but you and I both know that I was telling her the truth."

"She distrusts easily because she lies so much."

"When she repeated the comment about you being a thorn in her side, I had to try to find my voice to reply to her because she had shocked me into silence. When I recovered my voice, I asked very calmly if she would please put that in writing. She shouted at me, 'No I will not!' I can tell you, I have never been so shocked in my entire life. I said, 'Dr. Smith, are you telling me that Dr. Franklin is a thorn in your side? Dr. Claire Franklin?'"

Gerald sounded as if Jane had not only shocked him, but had hurt him as well. I remembered that he had supported her on some issues in the past, so this was probably more difficult for him than he let on. I asked him, "What'd she say then?"

"She told me that the conversation had ended and she hung up. I'm still trying to deal with this. I keep replaying it in my mind. I just can't believe that she said that about you!"

"I can. Now maybe you will believe more of what people have been saying to you about her all along. She can be very difficult." I was smiling to myself that now Gerald

Givens saw the side of Jane that so many of us had to live with as school district employees.

"Oh, my goodness!" he said with great emphasis. "She goes beyond being difficult. I can think of much stronger adjectives that would describe her exactly."

"I'm sure you can. I can think of a few myself. I do appreciate your calling to let me know what she said. What's your next step?"

"I'm going to talk with some people at the state level to see what we can do. I'll let you know what I find out."

"Thanks Gerald."

I could hardly wait to tell my mother what he said. For so long she had managed to find excuses for Jane while seeing all the negatives concerning Marlena. That changed after I told her what Gerald had told me. She was outraged. "You are a thorn in her side? How dare she say that you were the problem. She's been a thorn in a lot of sides in this county."

"Mom, I'm glad that you and Gerald both are now seeing this side of Jane. I've been trying to tell you that she's been a witch all along and you kept thinking it was just Marlena. I told you that it was virtually impossible to work with Jane. The woman will not tell the truth."

"That's alright. That is alright. She's going to regret being so mean to people and saying such ugly things. Justice will plumb the line. She'll get hers."

My mother had an uncanny way of accurately predicting some events. She could be very intuitive at times. I was hoping that she was accurate when she said that Jane would "get hers." And if she did "get hers", I hoped it would be as soon as possible, preferably the next day.

❖

I went by Louise's office the next morning and talked with her at length about how upset Gerald Givens had been when he spoke with me. She agreed with me that the incident would turn out to be a blessing in disguise in the long run because even though Jane had been negative toward me, she exposed her true feelings to someone who had been a supporter but who would now let others know what happened.

Louise added, "It's time that more people in the black community have a chance to see Jane for just who she is."

I said, "I don't think he would have been anymore surprised if someone had told him that Jane had been orchestrating a protest of the NAACP in Dane County. He was still in shock when he told me everything she said."

"I'm sure he was. Junior and Jane are respected in the black community because the average person doesn't know what they are really like. With Gerald Givens seeing the other side of her, it will go a long way in the fight to bring her down."

"Clearly she won't have the support that she would have had otherwise."

"No, she will not. And now Gerald is going to be able to question her himself based on his experience in this one situation."

"That's true. He won't be able to say as easily that people are exaggerating or spreading false rumors about Jane."

Louise emphasized her point. "He's had a major experience with her that I don't think he will ever forget. Jane may have burned the wrong bridge this time."

"I think you're right. Gerald said her attitude was so negative that he could not believe what he was hearing."

"He probably couldn't. He thought he was talking to Jane Smith, the woman who spoke for all people regardless of race. What he found out was that the person he thought of as Jane Smith does not exist ... never did."

"When Junior goes around to the political meetings grinning and trying to make everyone think what an open minded man he is, Gerald will know better. And, the people that Gerald talks to will know better."

"It's a no-win proposition for the Smiths."

"Junior probably told her she should never have spoken to Gerald like that."

I hadn't thought about that possibility. I asked her, "You think so?"

"I know them. I know how they operate. Jane, I'm sure, shot from the hip without thinking and then when she told Junior about it, I'll bet he didn't like it."

"You don't think so?"

"No, I know them too well. Junior is probably worried now that the NAACP is going to have blacks marching around the administration building singing *We Shall Overcome*. He definitely doesn't want that to happen."

"May be not, but I still think it's the best thing that could have happened. Especially since my mother now sees Jane for the type of person that she truly is. I couldn't have planned it to happen any better. Nothing that I could have said would have had the kind of effect that Gerald's experience with Jane has had on her. Thank goodness for Gerald Givens."

Louise smiled, "Thank goodness for your hot dog stand."

CHAPTER 22

Call it serendipity.

Call it synchronicity.

Call it providence.

Call it whatever you like, but this is what happened. I was in Target when I saw a familiar face in the aisle not far in front of me. He appeared to be taking his time shopping and was alone. It was Peter Jones. Just the man I needed to see. This was perfect.

There was no need for me to call him now. I could talk with him face to face outside of the boardroom and find out what I needed to know. I spoke as soon as I got close enough to say something without having to raise my voice.

"Mr. Jones … Peter … Hello."

"Oh hello Dr. Franklin. How are you?"

"I'm fine and you?"

"Great. Are you here shopping?"

"Yes, but I am so glad that I ran into you."

"You are? Why?"

"I need to talk with you and this is so much better than a phone call."

"You can always talk with me at the board meetings."

"No, this is not something we need to discuss at a board meeting."

He gave me a questioning look and said, "Well in that case, I'm glad we ran into each other."

"Do you remember some time ago when we talked about firing Dr. Smith?"

"Yes, I do. I remember telling you that I thought we needed to give her more time."

"You did indeed, but things have changed."

"How so?"

"I believe that if the vote were taken today it would be 7-2 to fire her."

"You've got to be kidding. Tell me you're joking."

"Look at me Peter. Do I look like I'm joking? This is serious business. It's not everyday that a board fires a superintendent."

"You are serious. Who are the two opposed? Ms. Washington and myself?"

"Yes, the two black members. That's the problem. The vote shouldn't be divided along racial lines. That's where you come in."

Peter stretched his eyes and pointed to himself as he asked, "Me?"

"Yes, you. Some of us think that you might be able to find it in your heart to vote with the majority."

"Then it will be 8-1."

I was glad that he was understood my point. "Exactly."

"You are really serious!" Peter was standing near a display in the aisle as he realized that I was serious and not joking. He literally fell over the top of the display with his upper body and just stayed there for a few minutes resting on the display before saying anything else.

At first he laughed, a nervous laugh. Then his eyes widened and he looked appalled. He said, "You mean to tell me, the board is planning to fire her without giving her time to correct the problems?"

"Correct which problems? The ones she created in the schools or the ones she's creating with the board?"

"I mean, if there are people on the board who think she should be fired, they need to have sufficient cause. You just don't fire a superintendent because she makes a few mistakes," he asserted as he got off of the display and stood looking at me with widened eyes.

"Peter, if you believe that she's only made a few mistakes, you must be one of only a handful of people in the county that feel that way. Look at all the notoriety she's brought into the county. People elected you and your fellow board members just for the sole purpose of getting rid of that woman."

"But to fire her? Have you talked with Ms. Washington? Celeste Washington?"

"No, I haven't talked with her personally about it. I do think the people who are looking at the votes discussed it with her, but the consensus is that she will remain loyal until the bitter end. No, no one thinks that she will ever vote to fire Jane Smith."

"How do you know all of this? Did some of the other board members tell you all of this?"

"No. As a matter of fact, I didn't get any of this from a board member. I got it from some people who are close to board members."

"I just don't know. I want to give her a chance."

"I know you do, but think about it. When the vote comes I hope you'll vote with the majority."

"You've given me a lot to think about for some time to come. I guess I should thank you for letting me know what's going on."

"If that's a thank-you, then you're welcome. I've got to go, but we'll talk about this again."

As it turned out, I didn't have a chance to discuss it with Peter again. That's why I know it was providential that we ran into each other that day in Target. He needed to hear all that I had to say, whether he agreed with me or not. He didn't need to be blindsided.

❖

I checked with Stacy at work periodically to obtain any information that I could on the board's progress in the direction of firing Dr. Smith. My desire was to hear that they were in the process of planning to take action soon. Each time that Stacy and I discussed the potential for firing Jane, there was always some reason why that couldn't be done anytime soon.

Stacy gave me the distinct impression that most of the board members had backed away from following through with their campaign promises, no matter what the school district employees were going through. She did assure me that Mark understood that the public was waiting patiently, but he was not going to be the one to try to force the board to take action.

I wondered what was going on with the chairman, Dewey Fowler, so I asked Stacy. She answered me cautiously as if trying to find the right words. "From what Mark has said Dewey is not actively pursuing termination at this point. He wants to give Jane more rope to hang herself."

My patience and understanding were wearing thin. "What more could Dewey be waiting for?"

"He wants something that is almost airtight."

"That sounds as if they are trying to build a case." I was getting more than a little miffed. "Let me make sure I understand what we're talking about with this. Dewey wants an airtight case and the voters who elected him want Jane fired."

"It's what the attorney has been saying to them."

"You mean Marvin Younkins?"

"Yes. He told them it could take a year or more before they had a solid case against her."

"He and the board fired three superintendents in less time than that over in Deerfield County. Why so long in Dane County?"

"Three in one year!" Stacy was astonished.

"I'm exaggerating, but they have fired several in just a few years. That's why I wanted Marvin Younkins for Dane County. I know what he can do."

"They are concerned about a lawsuit and how much it would cost them."

I never believed for one minute that Marvin Younkins couldn't find a way to legally fire Jane Smith. I was convinced he could help the board fire her and it wouldn't cost the district a fortune. "Is that the attorney or the board?"

"Maybe it is more the board than the attorney. I'm not sure. All I know is that Mark said it is much more involved than any of them realized."

"Have they forgotten that the superintendent serves at the pleasure of the board?"

"I don't think so."

"Well, I can tell you the waiting isn't getting any easier."

From that conversation, I surmised that we were going to be stuck with Jane Smith for at least another year or possibly longer. Thoughts of what could happen during another year of Jane's leadership gave me shudders.

So many people had already been hurt and their lives had been disrupted. There was still the pervasive fear district wide that employees and their children were at risk for possible retaliation solely for the 'crime' of disagreeing with Jane or her minions. It was hard to believe that it would take so much longer to do what needed to be done.

❖

The significance of what occurred next was made clear to me much later on. At the time it was just a part of information sharing. This is what happened. I saw Stacy in the break room several days after our conversation about firing Jane. I laughingly told her that I had been at the administration building and the receptionist had to buzz me into the office area. She sat up very erect and questioned me.

"What do you mean 'buzz' you into the office area?"

"You know, through the double doors."

Stacy folded her arms, exhaled loudly, and then responded slowly as if she wanted to be certain that I understood what she was asking.

"Claire, I know there are double doors, but tell me about 'buzzing' you in."

"Oh, I thought you knew," I explained still laughing. "They have a new security system in place now and you can't go through the double doors unless the receptionist pushes the buzzer."

"No, I did not know," Stacy snapped. "When did they add that feature to the district office?"

"I don't know. I assume it's because of the death threats that we heard Jane has been getting."

"Let me get this straight. Jane Smith is behind locked doors that can only be entered if the receptionist opens them for you?"

"Yes. That's exactly what is going on. Jane has a security system so no one can get in unless they are admitted by the woman on the front desk."

"Well if that doesn't beat all. Jane is safe behind her new security doors and our children are vulnerable in the schools."

I could tell that Stacy was not pleased about the security device at the administration building, but I was just telling her about it for the humor value. I never thought she would become angry. I had assumed that she would laugh along with me at Jane hiding out in the D.O. after putting us out of the building.

"Your children? Stacy you're not worried about your children are you?"

"Yes I'm worried. Jane and Junior sent threats out that board members with children needed to know that anyone could walk into a school and anything could happen to the children. Mark and Connie felt that the warning was directed to them."

"Oh no. I don't think they would try to harm your children." I was appalled.

"I don't know."

CHAPTER 23

A school board meeting was scheduled for the coming Tuesday night. I decided not to go because of what Stacy had said about the length of time it would take before they could plan to fire Jane Smith. So when Louise asked me that Tuesday afternoon if I was going to the board meeting, I immediately said that I was not planning to go.

"Claire, we need to go together. We haven't done that in a long time … ride together."

"I'm just a little put out with the board right now and I thought I would wait until next month to go."

"Please come with me, I really want to be at the meeting tonight and I don't want to go alone."

"Ok. I'll go. We can go together."

"Good. I'll pick you up at 6:45."

As soon as I got in Louise's car that evening, she turned to me and said, "They're going to fire Jane tonight!"

I thought she was joking. I just looked at her. She repeated it, "They're going to fire Jane tonight."

"What!" By this time she had made the U-turn in front of my house and was headed in the direction of the middle school for the board meeting.

"Louise? Are you serious?"

"Yes! That's why I wanted you to come tonight. You couldn't miss this meeting for the world! History is going to be made tonight in Dane County."

I remember throwing my head back and looking upward trying to fully understand what was happening. "Louise, are you sure? How do you know this?"

"Stacy told me this morning."

"Stacy! She told me that the attorney said it could take up to a year to fire her."

"That was before you told her about the security doors at the district office."

I was speechless. This experience was beginning to feel like a made-for-TV movie. I couldn't figure out how they could fire Jane after she added security doors at the D.O.

Louise continued, "Stacy was livid that Jane was safe behind those new security doors, but her children might have been in harm's way. So she lit into Mark and got him fired up. He called Dewey and then Dewey took it from there."

"I had no idea. I was just bringing her up to date on the latest with Jane's administration."

"I know. But, it was just what we needed to propel that board into the direction they should have taken months ago. It was the last straw."

"And they are really going to fire her tonight?"

Louise nodded. "Yes ma'am they are." She was past smiling. She was actually grinning. "In just a few hours Dr.

Jane Smith will be known as the former superintendent of Dane County School District."

I screamed, "This is too much! It's really going to happen tonight?"

When we reached the middle school Louise saw the head of the county teacher's union walking toward the building for the meeting. She called out to him and then rushed over to speak to him. They spoke briefly and she headed off to greet someone else. The guy from the teacher's union came up to me and said, "Louise just told me, they're going to fire Dr. Smith tonight." He had a huge smile on his face, obviously pleased at this turn of events.

I was concerned about the information getting out before the meeting so I cautioned him, "Please don't say anything to anyone until they actually fire her. I would hate for anything to go wrong."

"Oh, you don't have to worry about me," he said. " I won't say a word, but I'm going to get a front row seat. I don't want to miss a thing."

I went over to Louise and we walked inside. I followed her lead and we sat on the front row in the section that would give us the best view of the board. An elderly man came over to speak to Louise and she asked him to sit on the other side of her. The man was a city official from Cedar Hills and apparently knew Louise quite well. I overheard him ask her if things were going alright with Jane as superintendent.

Louise said to him, "Tonight will tell the story." The man was unaware of what was going to happen and kept talking.

While Louise and the man from Cedar Hills continued their conversation, I noticed that there was a lot of activity behind the area of the conference table that was going to be used by the board. There was a narrow hallway and I could see district personnel walking around briskly in that area. So I leaned over and interrupted Louise in order to get her opinion on all of the movement. Before she could answer, we saw Jane go up to Phil Carlton gesturing wildly. She looked frantic and he looked bewildered. He didn't seem to have the answer that she needed. By this time a tall man came out who walked with the air of authority.

Louise whispered, "That's the attorney, Marvin Younkins."

I looked at Marvin and thought that it was great to be able to put a face with the name. It was easy to see that he was accustomed to being in a position to make things happen.

Marvin Younkins walked over near where we were sitting and found Junior Smith. He put his arm around Junior's shoulder and Junior stood up. Marvin then walked him back to the hallway, leaning over talking to him the entire time. Then the two of them disappeared around the corner in the same direction that Jane had gone in when she and Phil were in the hallway.

The man from Cedar Hills asked Louise, "Wasn't that Junior I saw head back there?" Before she could answer his question, Junior and Jane appeared in the meeting room, coming from in the hallway in the back. Junior had his hand on Jane's waist, steering her to a chair so that he could sit beside her. Louise turned to the man form Cedar Hills and said, "We're going to have to be quiet. History is being made here tonight."

The board members came out and took their seats. Celeste and Peter looked strangely glum. There was seriousness, a solemnity that I had not witnessed before.

The board members were all business. I could tell, only because I knew so many of them well, that some of them were nervous. The room became eerily quiet. Everyone had stopped talking almost as if on cue.

I looked at Louise. I could hardly contain myself. I knew in those moments that it was about to happen. The board was finally going to take action against Jane. This caught me, and probably most of the people in the room, completely off guard. It was the one night so many of us had been waiting for. Just when we thought it would only happen at some distant future time, here we were … poised to watch the Dane County School Board of Trustees make history. This was awesome.

Dewey called the meeting to order. One look at the board and anyone familiar with procedures would recognize at once that something was amiss. The superintendent always, without exception, sits beside the board chairman. Tonight the superintendent was sitting in the audience with her husband.

Dr. Jane Smith was being dethroned.

Onlookers could certainly look at Jane's facial expression and know that something was not quite right. Her lips were pursed tightly together and her hands were folded in her lap. She was sitting rigidly erect with her head up in a haughty manner giving the impression that her steely posture alone could make a difference in what was about to transpire.

Once the meeting was called to order, a motion was made and then seconded to accept the minutes from the previous meeting. The motion passed unanimously with a show of hands. There was not a sound in the room except for Dewey's voice.

No rustling papers.

No one walking around.

No chairs moving.

No talking … not even whispering.

No coughing.

I will never forget what happened next. The scene played out like a thriller on the big screen. Mark Graves raised his hand and was recognized by Dewey. Mark then held up a piece of paper that he began to read from. He read a statement that was couched in specific legal language. It didn't matter. Everyone present understood the motion. They understood what he was saying. Mark was making a motion that the board terminate Dr. Jane Smith effective immediately. The motion contained legalese about her salary and compensation, but bottom line: The board was actually going to vote to fire Jane.

Mark's motion received a second from Connie Scott. Dewey stated that a motion had been made and seconded as read. He then opened the floor for discussion. There was none … not a word … not even from Celeste or Peter. That was surprising. I thought surely one or the other would have responded with comments in support of Jane to try to get the board to allow her more time or possibly reschedule the vote. But none of that happened. Instead Dewey moved on to the question: "Are you ready for the question? All in favor of the motion as read …."

The motion passed 7-2. Celeste Washington and Peter Jones voted against it. Victor Stone supported the majority. The board had voted along racial lines.

Susie Purle then made a motion to adjourn until Thursday evening at 7:30 p.m. with Howard Moore seconding. It passed unanimously without any debate.

A collective sigh went over the room. The people assembled relaxed and began to breathe normally again.

That's when I realized that we had all been trying hard not to breathe so that we wouldn't miss anything.

The man from Cedar Hills, sitting beside Louise, didn't move or say anything. He kept staring ahead as if in a trance. Louise turned to him and said that she hoped his question about how Jane was doing had been answered. He looked at her and nodded in the affirmative. Then he got up, said good night and left. Louise turned to me and smiled. I wanted to jump up and down and celebrate.

Instead, Louise and I went up to thank the board members. I shook hands with each one of the seven members who had voted to terminate Jane and let them know individually that I thought that what they had done was for the good of the school district and Dane County as a whole.

Then I approached Peter and Celeste who were standing together. Celeste was so angry the color had changed in her face. She said that something needed to be done about the board firing Jane. Peter, who was perspiring heavily, agreed with her. I shook their hands and made a vague remark, something like, "We'll talk later." I don't remember my exact words, but I do remember that Louise was suddenly beside me telling me that she was ready to leave.

On the walk to Louise's car she said that we were driving over to Shoney's in the Riverplains area. That was where the West Sandhills board members had planned to go to celebrate Jane's firing. I felt almost giddy. The representative from the teacher's union came up and was smiling broadly. He laughed and said he just wanted to thank Louise for telling him what was going to happen and that she just might have prevented a heart attack with the warning. We all laughed and then he left, still smiling.

The air outside felt light and full of promise. It still felt like a dream. The board had fired Jane Smith! Little did I know when I agreed to attend the board meeting with Louise that night that I would witness history being made in Dane County. People were still standing outside in small groups laughing and talking. Reality had set in and the celebration was on.

As soon as we got in the car I asked Louise, "The truth. How long did you know about this?"

"I'm serious. Stacy just told me this morning."

"Suppose I had refused to come to the meeting tonight. I would have missed the whole thing."

"No, you were coming if I had to tell you everything ahead of time. I was not going to let you miss this meeting tonight."

"I still can't believe it happened!"

"Believe it. Jane is no longer our superintendent."

"Do you think that Junior and Jane will try to undo this by Thursday night?"

"There's nothing they can do. The attorney handled all the legal issues. This guy is probably one of the best school board attorneys in the state."

"I know."

"I don't know how they got him, but it was the best thing that could have happened. Otherwise we might not be on our way to Shoney's to celebrate."

"You're right. The board had to get a real school board attorney and not one who worked for the district in addition to handling traffic court, divorces, and adoptions."

"We need to call Madelyn. Use my car phone."

Madelyn was a mutual friend who had worked with Jane many years ago and ended up retiring to get away from the current administration. She was cynical and opinionated, but we loved her.

I got Madelyn on the phone, "Hi, this is Claire. How are you? I hope you haven't gone to bed." Madelyn supplemented her income by delivering newspapers and usually went to be early so that she could be up at 4:30 a.m. to go to the distribution center.

I continued, "I'm with Louise. We just left the board meeting and we're headed to Shoney's in Riverplains. We have some news for you! You're not going to believe what happened at the board meeting tonight!"

Of course Madelyn wanted to know what had happened. I told her, "The board fired Jane!"

"They did what?" She was shocked.

"They fired Jane! Can you believe that? We're so excited! Do you want to meet us at Shoney's?"

"It'll only take a few minutes to put something on and I'm on my way!"

"Ok. We'll meet you there."

After I hung up, I asked Louise if there was anyone else she wanted me to call, and then I remembered my mother. I called her, "Hi Mom. I hope you're sitting down." I laughed and explained, "That's so you can jump up and cheer at what I'm about to tell you. They fired Jane Smith at the board meeting tonight!"

"Oh, thank God. I've been praying for the board to do the right thing."

"Well Louise and I are headed over to Shoney's to meet some people and celebrate."

"That's great. Enjoy yourselves. I'll see you later and you can give me all of the details."

❖

Louise and I were among the first of the celebrants to arrive at Shoney's. We were seated in a booth midway the restaurant with a good view of the entrance so that we could see who came in. Not long after the waitress brought our coffee, Madelyn came rushing in with a gigantic smile. We hugged and she joined us in the booth. "Claire! Louise! I can't wait to hear everything that happened. This is worth getting out of bed for. I just can't believe it!"

"Oh I know," I agreed. "It seems that we waited for so long for this to happen and then the board fires Jane."

Madelyn said very matter-of-factly, "Everyone knew Jane had no business being superintendent. The woman was too spiteful to do her job. She was always trying to pay somebody back for something. She and Junior could hold a grudge for years."

"That's what I heard," I reported. "Someone told me that they would act like a disagreement was over, giving you enough time to let your guard down and then they got you back."

"That's the way they operate," Louise added.

By this time the Riverplains contingent from the board arrived, accompanied by their families and friends. Louise clapped loudly and Madelyn and I both followed suit. The restaurant then broke out into wild applause. Susie Purle, Howard Moore, and Greg Townsend waved their hands and thanked their supporters. Susie spoke for the group by saying that they had acted in what they felt was the best interest of the school district. She went on to explain that the board members were not at liberty to discuss the specifics of the termination until all the legal matters were handled. It was possible that Jane Smith might decide to sue.

None of that put a damper on the mood or the celebration. As soon as Susie stopped talking it seemed as if an invisible volume control knob had been turned up because the place became incredibly noisy with laughter and loud voices. The party spirit was infectious with everyone in the restaurant that night getting caught up in the fun and frivolity.

It ended way too soon. Before we knew it an hour or so had passed and it was time to leave. Louise and I found the board members, thanked them again, and said good night. We told Madelyn good night in the parking lot and drove back toward Lucien Heights.

Louise and I joked in the car about the events of earlier in the evening. We analyzed Jane's behavior during the time she was running around in the back hallway and the way she went to Phil Carlton, who didn't appear to have been able to calm her down. We talked about the anger that Celeste and Peter expressed and how hard it would be for them to be mollified.

No matter what we talked about, it still felt like a dream. It was such an incredible experience.

❖

Another phase of the night began for me as soon as I returned home. My mother had to hear a detailed description of everything that had occurred beginning with my leaving for the board meeting with Louise. The feelings that I had recounting the events of that night defy description. I felt elation, relief, joy, and so much positive energy that I had an overall feeling of 'all is well with the world'. We had a mini celebration, my mother and I, and danced around laughing and feeling good about the firing.

With the joyfulness there was the anticipation of better days to come … freedom of speech … freedom of expression … freedom from fear … freedom for honesty and openness. Surely the best was yet to come.

My phone was ringing nonstop until about three o'clock in the morning. That was the last call that I received. It was from a friend of mine who was a guidance counselor at Lucien Heights High. She called for confirmation of the firing. Having been a victim of Jane's abuse of power, she was guarded in her query initially, "Claire, I heard something tonight and I knew you would be the one person who would tell me the truth."

"What did you hear?"

"I heard that the board fired Jane Smith. Is that true?"

"It is indeed. I was there. I witnessed the entire thing."

"Oh! Thank goodness! I knew you would know exactly what happened. She's really gone?"

'Yes she is. The vote was 7-2 to terminate her with Celeste and Peter opposing."

"They didn't know any better. Jane had them fooled, but they'll find out how people really felt now that they've fired her. The truth will come out. They will be amazed at how intimidated and terrified people were of Jane and her flunkies."

"I know. It's like a tremendous burden has been lifted."

"People won't know how to behave with the threat of Jane gone. What's that old expression? Free till they're fool? That's it. They're going to be free until they're crazy. They won't know what to do with themselves. I would go out now and celebrate myself if it wasn't so late."

"You can celebrate tomorrow night. No, as late as it is, it's already tomorrow! You can celebrate tonight!"

"That's right. Oh, I'm glad that we had a chance to talk. Thank you so much! I can't wait to get to Lucien Heights High in a few hours. I can't wait to see the teachers and the administrators. I don't know anyone in the school that liked Jane. If it wasn't a shame, they'd probably have a rally in the gym, but that would be in poor taste."

I laughed and reminded her that it was late, but that we could talk later in the evening. We said goodnight and I had chance to go to bed, at last.

❖

Near the end of the school day on Wednesday, less than 24 hours after the school board terminated Dr. Jane Smith, I heard from a district employee that several of the teachers at Lucien Heights High School had been observed dancing around in the hall that morning singing "Ding dong, the witch is dead…."

38266448R00133

Made in the USA
Lexington, KY
30 December 2014